Christopher Marlowe's The Massacre at Paris: A Retelling

David Bruce

Published by David Bruce, 2022.

CHRISTOPHER MARLOWE'S THE MASSACRE AT PARIS: A RETELLING

First edition. July 17, 2022.

Copyright © 2022 David Bruce.

ISBN: 979-8201132705

Written by David Bruce.

Table of Contents

Cover Photograph for Christopher Marlowe's *The Massacre at Paris*: A Retelling

***

COVER PHOTO

https://pixabay.com/en/woman-old-senior-desperation-grief-1246587/

Dedicated to Carl Eugene Bruce and Josephine Saturday Bruce

***

Educate Yourself
Read Like A Wolf Eats
Be Excellent to Each Other
Books Then, Books Now, Books Forever

***

In this retelling, as in all my retellings, I have tried to make the work of literature accessible to modern readers who may lack some of the knowledge about mythology, religion, and history that the literary work's contemporary audience had.

Do you know a language other than English? If you do, I give you permission to translate this book, copyright your translation, publish or self-publish it, and keep all the royalties for yourself. (Do give me credit, of course, for the original retelling.)

I would like to see my retellings of classic literature used in schools, so I give permission to the country of Finland (and all other countries) to buy (or get free) one copy of this eBook and give copies to all students forever. I also give permission to the state of Texas (and all other states) to buy (or get free) one copy of this eBook and give copies to all students forever. I also give permission to all teachers to buy (or get free) one copy of this eBook and give copies to all students forever.

Teachers need not actually teach my retellings. Teachers are welcome to give students copies of my eBooks as background material. For example, if they are teaching Homer's *Iliad* and *Odyssey*, teachers are welcome to give students copies of my *Virgil's* Aeneid: *A Retelling in Prose* and tell students, "Here's another ancient epic you may want to read in your spare time."

CAST OF CHARACTERS

Male Characters

Charles IX, King of France. Born 27 June 1550. Reigned from 5 December 1560 to 30 May 1574. His mother, Catherine the Queen-Mother, wielded much power.

Duke of Anjou, his brother, later King Henry III of France. Born 19 September 1551. Reigned from 30 May 1574 to 2 August 1589. He was attacked on 1 August 1589 and died the following day. King Henry III was the last French King of the House of Valois. Before dying, King Henry III of France named the King of Navarre — aka King Henry III the Great of Navarre — as his heir.

The King of Navarre, later King Henry IV of France. He was the first French King of the House of Bourbon. (The word "House" means "Family.") Before becoming King of France, he reigned as King of Poland from 16 May 1573 to 12 May 1575.

Minions of the Duke of Anjou:

• Duke of Joyeux.

• Mugeroun.

Duke of Epernoun, Friend to the Duke of Anjou, who became King Henry III. Attendant to Charles IX of France.

Duke of Guise. A Catholic. He helped plan the Saint Bartholomew's Day Massacre, which started on 24 August 1572 and then spread and lasted for over two months. He was murdered on 23 December 1588. He is Duke Henry I of Guise. In 1576, he formed the Catholic League.

Brothers to the Duke of Guise:

• Cardinal of Lorraine. He is Louis of Lorraine and is also known as Louis II, Cardinal of Guise. He was born on 6 July 1555 and murdered on 24 December 1588.

• Duke of Dumaine.

Son to the Duke of Guise.

Followers of the Duke of Guise:

- Gonzago.
- Retes.
- Mountsorrell.

King Henry III of Navarre, later King Henry IV of France. Born 13 December 1553. Reigned as King of Navarre from 9 June 1572 to 14 May 1610. Reigned as King of France from 2 August 1589 to 14 May 1610. Navarre is a Huguenot noble; he is a leader of the Huguenots.

Prince of Condé. A leader of the Huguenots.

Lord High Admiral. His name is Gaspard de Coligny, seigneur de Châtillon. Assassinated on 24 August 1572. A leader of the Huguenots.

The Admiral's servant.

Friends of King of Navarre:

- Pleshé.
- Bartus.

Cossin, Captain of the Guard.

Victims in the Massacre:

- Loreine.
- Seroune.
- Petrus Ramus. A philosopher and logician. He was also a convert to Protestantism. Killed on 26 August 1572.

Taleus, friend to Ramus.

Female Characters

Catherine, Queen-Mother of France. Her name is Catherine de' Medici. Her children include Charles IX, King of France; the Duke of Anjou (later King Henry III); and Margaret, Queen of Navarre.

Joan, Old Queen of Navarre. Queen-Mother to the King of Navarre.

Margaret, Queen of Navarre, daughter to Catherine, wife to King of Navarre. Sister of Charles IX, King of France. She was a Roman Catholic. Before her marriage, she was known as Margaret of Valois.

Duchess of Guise.

Wife to Seroune.

Maid to the Duchess of Guise.

Minor Characters
Apothecary.
Two Lords of Poland.
Cutpurse.
Friar.
Surgeon.
The English Agent.
Three Murderers.
Protestants, Schoolmasters, Soldiers, Attendants, and Messengers.
NOTES:

The massacre referred to in the title is the St. Bartholomew's Day Massacre, which occurred in 1572 during the French Wars of Religion. In this massacre, Catholics targeted Huguenots (French Protestants). The massacre began just before dawn on 24 August 1572 (St. Bartholomew's Day) in Paris. The violence spread from Paris and continued for over two months.

Christopher Marlowe, as did many other Elizabethan playwrights, collapses time. The events depicted after the massacre seem to take place very quickly, but they actually took place over years. The St. Bartholomew's Day Massacre began just before dawn on 24 August 1572, and King Henry III of Navarre became King Henry IV of France on 2 August 1589.

Joan, Old Queen of Navarre, was actually Queen-Regent of Navarre from 25 May 1555 to 9 June 1572. In history, she actually died two months before her son married Margaret of Valois, although in Marlowe's play she dies soon after the marriage. In Scene 2, when the Duke of Guise talks about poisoning the Queen of Navarre, he means Joan, not Margaret. In Marlowe's play, Joan is murdered; in history, she died of natural causes (but rumors stated that she was poisoned).

As always, we read Elizabethan history plays for drama, not history. Elizabethan playwrights, including Shakespeare, see no problems in changing history in order to serve dramatic needs.

Editors divide Marlowe's play into different numbers of scenes. This book has 25 scenes.

Probably the play as we have it is a memorial reconstruction. The original play would most likely have been much longer.

Scene 19 in this retelling combines the words of the undated octavo edition and the words of the Collier Leaf, which may be genuine and which contains additional passages. The Collier Leaf does not include the soldier's line about "if this gear hold."

Anywhere from 5,000 to 30,000 people died in France during the massacre. Some estimates are higher or lower.

CHAPTER 1

[SCENE ONE]

King Charles IX of France, Catherine the Queen-Mother, the King of Navarre, the Prince of Condé, the Lord High Admiral, and the Queen of Navarre, with others, stood outside the Notre-Dame Cathedral at Paris.

The date was 18 August 1572, and the King of Navarre, not yet nineteen years old, had just married Margaret of Valois: They were now King Henry and Queen Margaret of Navarre. The King of Navarre was a Huguenot (French Protestant), and Queen Margaret was a member of a Roman Catholic family. Because of the marriage, King Charles IX of France and the King of Navarre were now brothers-in-law.

The marriage was arranged in part in an attempt to stop the discord between Protestants and Catholics, and the marriage ceremony was designed to satisfy both religions.

The marriage did not stop the discord between Protestants and Catholics. In a few days — just before dawn on August 24 — the Saint Bartholomew's Day Massacre would start.

King Charles IX of France said, "King of Navarre (who is now my honorable brother-in-law), Prince Condé, and my good Lord High Admiral, I wish this union and religious league and sacred alliance, knit in these hands of the King of Navarre and Margaret, thus joined in nuptial rites, may not dissolve until death dissolves our lives. And I wish that the natural sparks of princely love, which kindled first this desire in our hearts, may in the future be fed with fuel in our progeny."

The King of Navarre replied, "The many favors that your grace has shown from time to time, but especially in this, shall bind me forever to your highness' will in what Catherine the Queen-Mother or your grace commands."

King Charles IX of France was only twenty-two years old, and he had become King of France at the age of ten. His mother, Catherine the Queen-Mother, had wielded much power when he was an adolescent King, and she still had much influence and wielded much power.

"Thanks, son-in-law Navarre," Catherine the Queen-Mother said. "You see we love you well, we who link you in marriage with our daughter here; and, as you know, our difference in religion might be a means to cross you in your love."

The King of Navarre was a Huguenot (French Protestant), while Catherine the Queen-Mother was a Catholic.

King Charles IX of France said to his mother, "Well, madam, let that rest. And now, my lords, with the marriage rites performed, we think it is good to go and complete the rest of the ceremonies with the hearing of a holy mass. Sister, I think you will bear us company."

His sister, Margaret, now Queen of Navarre, who was also a Catholic, replied, "I will, my good lord."

"Those who will not go, my lords, may stay," King Charles IX of France said. "Come, mother, let us go to honor this solemn ceremony of marriage."

Catherine the Queen-Mother thought, *This marriage I'll dissolve with blood and cruelty.*

King Charles IX of France, Catherine the Queen-Mother, and Queen Margaret of Navarre exited to attend the mass.

The King of Navarre, the Prince of Condé, and the Lord High Admiral stayed. Since they were Protestants, they would not attend the mass.

They began to discuss politics, and especially the actions of the Duke of Guise, who was a Catholic and who was virulently anti-Protestant.

"Prince Condé, and my good Lord High Admiral," the King of Navarre said, "now the Duke of Guise may storm, but he will do us little hurt because we have King Charles IX of France and Catherine the Queen-Mother on our sides. They will stop the malice of his evil-intending heart that seeks to murder all Protestants.

"You must have heard of how the Duke of Guise declared recently that if King Charles IX had given his consent, then all the Protestants who are in Paris should have been murdered the other night."

"My lord," the Lord High Admiral replied, "I marvel that the aspiring Duke of Guise would dare under any circumstances, without the King's consent, to venture to attempt such dangerous things."

"My lord, you need not marvel at the Duke of Guise," Prince Condé said, "for what he does in murder, mischief, or in tyranny, the Pope will ratify."

The Protestants greatly mistrusted many Catholics and Pope Gregory XIII. Prince Condé believed that the Duke of Guise had the support of the Pope, and so the Duke of Guise would be willing to attack the Protestants even without King Charles IX's support.

The King of Navarre said, "But He Who sits and rules above the clouds hears and sees the prayers of the just, and will revenge the blood of innocents, that the Duke of Guise has slain by treason of his heart, and brought by murder to their untimely ends."

The Lord High Admiral said to the King of Navarre, "My lord, but did you notice how the Cardinal of Lorraine and the Duke of Dumaine, both of whom are the Duke of Guise's brothers, stormed at these your nuptial rites, because the House of Bourbon now comes in, and joins your lineage to the crown of France?"

Through his marriage, the King of Navarre now had a claim through the female line as an heir to the throne of France. Queen Margaret of Navarre was a Valois, a member of the French royal family. She was the sister of King Charles IX of France.

If the direct male line of the Kings of France were to end, it was possible for the King of Navarre, a member of the House of Bourbon, to also become King of France. If that were to happen, he would be France's first Bourbon King.

The King of Navarre said, "And that's the reason that Duke Guise so frowns at us, and racks his brains to find a way to catch us in his trap, which he has pitched within his deadly net.

"Come, my lords, let's go to the church, and pray that God may still defend the right of France, and make his gospel flourish in this land."

CHAPTER 2

Alone in a room in his house, the Duke of Guise said to himself, "If ever Hymen, the god of marriage, loured at marriage rites, and had his altars decked with dim and dusky lights, and if ever sun stained heaven with bloody clouds, and made it look with terror on the world, and if ever day were turned to ugly night, and the night given the semblance of the hue of hell, then this day, this hour, this fatal night, shall fully show the fury of them all."

He called, "Apothecary!"

The apothecary entered the room and asked, "My Lord?"

"Now I shall test and reward to the full the love you bear the House of Guise," the Duke of Guise replied. "Where are those perfumed gloves that I sent to be poisoned? Have you poisoned them yet? Speak! Will every act of smelling them breed a pang of death?"

In this society, gloves were expensive, and they were perfumed.

The apothecary pointed to the gloves and said, "See where they are, my good lord. Anyone who smells them dies."

"Then you remain resolute?" the Duke of Guise asked.

"I do, and I am resolute, my lord, in what your grace commands, until my death," the apothecary replied.

"Thanks, my good friend," the Duke of Guise replied. "I will requite your love and friendship. Go, then, present the poisoned gloves to the Queen of Navarre, for she is that huge blemish that is always in front of us and that foments these upstart heresies of Protestantism in France."

By the Queen of Navarre, he meant the old Queen: Joan. The Duke of Guise believed that she supported what he called Protestant heresies. The Queen-Mother Joan was Calvinist; she was a Huguenot.

The Duke of Guise continued, "Be gone, my friend, present the poisoned gloves to her immediately."

The apothecary exited.

The Duke of Guise called, "Soldier!"

A soldier entered the room and asked, "My lord?"

"Now go forth, and play your tragic part," the Duke of Guise said. "Stand in some window, opening near the street, and when you see the Lord High Admiral ride by, discharge your musket, and ensure his death. And then I'll reward you with a store of coins."

"I will, my lord," the soldier replied, and he exited.

The Duke of Guise began to talk to himself:

"Now, Guise, those deeply engendered thoughts of yours begin to burst abroad and spread on all sides those never dying flames that cannot be extinguished but by blood.

"Often I have thought and at last have learned that peril is the chiefest way to happiness, and that resolution is the best path to honor.

"What glory is there in a common good that hangs like easily plucked fruit for every peasant to achieve? I like best that which flees beyond my reach.

"Set me to scale the high pyramids, and on a pyramid set the diadem of France. I'll either rend the pyramid with my fingernails to nothing, or mount to the top with my aspiring wings, even if my downfall would be the deepest hell.

"The crown of France is what I want.

"For this I stay awake, when others think I sleep.

"For this I wait, although I scorn to wait on anything or anyone else.

"For this, my quenchless thirst, whereon I build, has often debated and wrangled with the kindred to the King.

"For this, this head of my plots, this heart of mine imagines, and this hand and sword of mine fully executes, matters of importance aimed at by many, yet understood by none."

In this society, the heart was considered the seat of imagination. The Duke of Guise's heart had imagined the goal he wished to achieve. He was executing actions designed to make him King of France, although no one understood that.

The Duke of Guise continued:

"For this has heaven engendered me from earth.

"For this, this earth sustains my body's weight, and with this weight I'll furnish myself with a crown, or I will weary all the world with seditions.

"For this, from Spain the stately, princely, arrogant Catholics send me Indian gold to coin French crowns.

"For this I have a largess from the Pope, a pension, and a religious dispensation."

A largess is a monetary gift. A pension is regular payments of money. The religious dispensation gave the Duke of Guise permission to perform actions forbidden by ecclesiastical law.

The Duke of Guise continued:

"And by using that privilege of religious dispensation, my political cunning has framed and shaped religion as if it were a building material; I am making religion serve political expediency.

"Religion: *O diabole*! Oh, the devil!

"Oh, I am ashamed, however unashamed I seem, to think a word of such a simple sound should be made the foundation of so great matter — my ambitious scheme! It is religion that shall make me King of France!

"The uncontrolled pleasure of the gentle King Charles IX of France has weakened his body and will waste his realm unless I repair what he ruins."

"As if he were a child, I daily win him with words, so that in practice he barely bears the name of his position; he is King in name only.

"I execute, and he sustains the blame.

"Catherine the Queen-Mother works wonders for my sake, and entombs and commits the welfare of France to my love, rifling the bowels of her treasury, to supply my wants and my necessity.

"Paris has in full five hundred colleges, such as monasteries, priories, abbeys, and halls, wherein are thirty thousand able men, besides a thousand sturdy student Catholics. And furthermore, of my knowledge, in one cloister dwell five hundred fat Franciscan friars and priests:

"I have all this, and more, if more may be included, to bring the will of our desires to an end. I have all of this to use to accomplish my goal of becoming King of France.

"So then, Duke of Guise, since you control so much — you have all the cards within your hands, to shuffle or cut — take this as a surest thing, that, right or wrong, you deal yourself a King.

"Yes, but Navarre, Navarre. It is only a nook of France, yet sufficient for such a petty King, a King who, with a rabblement of his Protestant heretics, blinds Europe's eyes, and troubles our estate — the realm of France.

"The King of Navarre ... him will we" — he put his hand on his sword and then continued, "but first let's pursue those in France who hinder our progression to the soon-to-be possession of the crown.

"As Caesar said to his soldiers, so say I, 'Those who hate me I will learn to loathe.'

"Give me a look that, when I bend my eyebrows and frown, pale death may walk in the furrows of my face.

"Give me a hand that with a grasp may grip and lay hold of the world.

"Give me an ear to hear what my detractors say.

"Give me a royal seat, a scepter, and a crown that when people behold it, they may become like men who stand and gaze at the sun — let the sight of my crown strike them blind.

"The plot is laid, and things shall come to pass where resolution strives for victory. My resolution shall result in my victory."

CHAPTER 3

The King of Navarre and Queen Margaret of Navarre were in a street with Joan (the King's Queen-Mother), the Prince of Condé, and the Lord High Admiral. They were on a street between the Louvre and the lodging of the Lord High Admiral.

The apothecary entered, carrying the poisoned gloves, and he gave them to old Queen Joan, saying, "Madam, I beg your grace to accept this simple gift."

"Thanks my good friend," old Queen Joan said. "Wait. Take this reward for yourself."

She gave him some money.

"I humbly thank your majesty," the apothecary said, and then he exited.

"I think the gloves have a very strong perfume, whose scent makes my head ache," old Queen Joan said.

Her son the King of Navarre asked, "Does your grace know the man who gave the gloves to you?"

"Not well," old Queen Joan replied, "but I do remember such a man."

"Your grace was ill advised to take the gloves, then," the Lord High Admiral said, "considering these dangerous times."

"Help, son Navarre!" old Queen Joan said. "I am poisoned!"

"May the heavens forbid your highness such misfortune!" Queen Margaret said.

The King of Navarre said, "The recent grounds we have had for suspecting the Duke of Guise might well have moved your highness to be careful how you did concern yourself with such dangerous gifts."

"It is too late, my lord, if that is true, to blame her highness," Queen Margaret said, "but I hope it is only some natural illness and not poison that makes her sick."

"Oh, no, sweet Margaret," old Queen Joan said, "the fatal poison works within my head! My brainpan breaks! My heart faints! I die!"

She died.

"My mother poisoned here before my face!" the King of Navarre said. "Oh, gracious God, what times are these? Oh, grant, sweet God, that my days may end with hers, so that I with her may die and live again in heaven!"

"Don't let this sorrowful event, my dearest lord — my soul is massacred because of your mother's death — infect your gracious breast with a fresh supply of what will aggravate our sudden misery."

"Come, my lords, let us bear her body away from here and see it honored with just solemnity," the Lord High Admiral said.

The Lord High Admiral and some others picked up old Queen Joan's body and started to carry it away. As they were leaving, from a window the soldier shot his musket at the Lord High Admiral and hit him. The soldier then fled.

The Prince of Condé asked, "Are you hurt, my Lord High Admiral?"

"Yes, my good lord," the Lord High Admiral replied. "I am shot through the arm."

"We are betrayed!" the King of Navarre said. "Come, my lords, and let us go tell King Charles IX of France about this."

"These malefactors are the cursed Guisians, who seek our death," the Lord High Admiral said. "Oh, fatal was this marriage to us all."

They carried away the body of old Queen Joan.

CHAPTER 4

King Charles IX of France, Catherine the Queen-Mother, the Duke of Guise, the Duke of Anjou (the King's brother), and the Duke of Dumaine (the Duke of Guise's brother) met together in a room in the palace. The purpose of the meeting was to convince King Charles IX to approve of the massacre of Protestants that Catherine and the Duke of Guise were planning.

Catherine the Queen-Mother said, "My noble son, and princely Duke of Guise, now we have got the doomed, straggling deer — the Protestants — within the compass of a deadly trap, and we may perform what we recently decided to do."

King Charles IX of France replied, "Madam, it will be noted and stigmatized through the world chiefly as a bloody and tyrannical action since the Protestants justly claim their protection under safety of our word: They have the word of me the King that they will be safe."

The Protestants had come to Paris for the marriage of the King of Navarre and Margaret of Valois with the promise from King Charles IX of France that they would be safe.

King Charles IX of France continued, "Besides, my heart melts that noble men, corrupted only in religion, as well as ladies of honor, knights, and gentlemen, should, because of their religious conscience, taste such ruthless ends."

"Although gentle, noble, courteous minds should pity others' pains," the Duke of Anjou said, "yet the wisest will note their own griefs, and rather seek to scourge their enemies than be themselves base subjects to the whip."

"I think, my lord," the Duke of Guise said, "that the Duke of Anjou has well advised your highness to consider the thing and to choose to seek your country's good rather than to pity or relieve these upstart heretics."

"I hope these reasons may serve my princely son to take some care — some preventive action — for fear of enemies," Catherine the Queen-Mother said.

"Well, madam, I refer this matter to your majesty, and to my relative here, the Duke of Guise," King Charles IX of France said. "What you decide, I will ratify and formally sanction."

"I give thanks to my princely son," Catherine the Queen-Mother said.

She then asked, "Tell me, Guise, what order will you set down for the massacre?"

The Duke of Guise replied, "This is the plan, madam. They who shall be actors in this massacre shall wear white crosses on their light helmets and tie white linen scarves around their arms. Whatever man lacks these, and is suspected of heresy, shall die, be he King or Emperor. Then I'll have a peal of large cannon sound from the tower, at which all the actors in this massacre shall issue out, and be on the streets preparing to be a net to catch people. And then once the watchword is given, a bell shall ring; when they hear the bell, they shall begin to kill, and never cease until that bell shall cease. Then they shall rest for a while."

A servant of the Lord High Admiral entered the room. He was acting as a messenger.

King Charles IX of France asked, "What is it now? What news do you bring?"

"If it please your grace, the Lord High Admiral, while riding in the streets, was traitorously shot, and he most humbly entreats your majesty to visit him, sick in his bed."

"Messenger, tell him I will see him immediately," King Charles IX of France said.

The messenger exited.

King Charles IX of France asked, "What shall we do now with the Lord High Admiral?"

"It's best that your majesty go visit him, and act as if all were well," Catherine the Queen-Mother replied.

"OK," King Charles IX of France said. "I will go visit the Lord High Admiral."

"And I will go make arrangements for his death," the Duke of Guise said.

CHAPTER 5

King Charles IX of France was visiting the Lord High Admiral, who was in bed in his lodging. Some attendants were present, as was Cossin, the Captain of the Guard.

King Charles IX of France asked, "How is my Lord High Admiral? Have villains in the street hurt him? I vow and swear as King of France to find and to repay the man with death — with death delayed and torments never before used — who dared to presume, for hope of any gain, to hurt the noble man whom his sovereign loves."

"Ah, my good lord, the malefactors are the followers of the Duke of Guise — the Guisians — who seek to massacre our guiltless lives!" the Lord High Admiral said.

"Assure yourself, my good Lord Admiral," King Charles IX of France said, "that I deeply sorrow for the treacherous wrong done to you, and so assure yourself that I am not more safe and secure myself than I am careful that your life should be preserved."

He then ordered, "Cossin, take twenty of our strongest guards, and under your direction see that they keep all treacherous violence away from our noble friend, repaying all attempts on our friend with immediate death upon the cursed breakers of our peace."

He then said, "And so be patient, good Lord High Admiral, and I will visit you every hour."

"I humbly thank your royal majesty," the Lord High Admiral said.

CHAPTER 6

[SCENE SIX]

The Duke of Guise, the Duke of Anjou, the Duke of Dumaine, Gonzago, Retes, Mountsorrell, and some soldiers talked together just before the massacre, which would begin just before dawn on this day of 24 August 1572 (St. Bartholomew's Day) in Paris.

The Duke of Guise said, "Anjou, Dumaine, Gonzago, Retes, swear by the silver-white crosses on your light helmets to kill all whom you suspect of heresy. Kill all the Protestants."

"I swear by this cross to be unmerciful," the Duke of Dumaine said.

"I am disguised," the Duke of Anjou said, "and no one knows who I am, and therefore I intend to murder all I meet."

"And so will I," Gonzago said.

"And I," Retes said.

"Go, then!" the Duke of Guise said. "Break into the Lord High Admiral's house."

"Yes, let the Lord High Admiral be first killed," Retes said.

"The Lord High Admiral, chief standard bearer to the Lutherans, shall in the beginning of this massacre be murdered in his bed," the Duke of Guise said.

He ordered, "Gonzago, conduct them there, and then beset his house, so that not a man in his house may live."

"That charge of besetting the house is mine," the Duke of Anjou said.

By "charge," he meant "responsibility." Ironically, one meaning of "charge" is "responsibility for taking care of someone."

The Duke of Anjou and the people with him headed toward the Lord High Admiral's house.

The Duke of Anjou continued, "Switzers, keep in the streets, and the King's guard shall stand at each corner."

The Switzers are Swiss guards; they are mercenaries.

"Come, sirs, follow me," Gonzago said.

Gonzago and some soldiers exited.

The Duke of Anjou said, "Cossin, the Captain of the Guard that is supposed to protect the Lord High Admiral, placed there by my brother King Charles IX of France, will betray his lord."

Cossin would definitely betray the Lord High Admiral, a leader of the French Protestants.

Arriving at the Lord High Admiral's lodging with the Duke of Guise and others, the Duke of Anjou said, "Now, Guise, Catholics shall flourish once again. The head being off, the members cannot stand."

"But look, my lord," Retes said, "there's some people in the Admiral's house."

He could see them through a window. Gonzago and some soldiers were already in the house. They were upstairs, where the Lord High Admiral was in bed.

"This is a lucky time to arrive!" the Duke of Anjou said. "Come, let us stay outside and keep this lane, and slay the Lord High Admiral's servants who shall come out of the house."

"Where is the Lord High Admiral?" Gonzago asked in the lodging.

Seeing them and realizing that they wanted to kill him, the Lord High Admiral, wounded and in bed, said, "Oh, let me pray before I die!"

"Then pray to our lady," Gonzago said. "Kiss this cross."

"Our lady" is Mary the Virgin Mother. The cross Gonzago meant was the one formed by the blade, hilt, and pommel of his sword.

Gonzago stabbed the Lord High Admiral, who prayed as he died, "Oh, God, forgive my sins!"

Because the Lord High Admiral was a Protestant, he prayed directly to God. As a Catholic, Gonzago had advised him to use an intermediary: Mary the Virgin Mother.

From the street outside, the Duke of Guise called, "Gonzago, is he dead?"

Gonzago went to a window and replied, "Yes, my lord."

"Then throw his body down," the Duke of Guise said.

Gonzago dragged the body to the window and threw it down.

"Now, kinsman, view the body well," the Duke of Anjou advised. "It may be it is someone else, and the Lord High Admiral has escaped."

The Duke of Guise wiped away blood from the corpse's face and said, "Kinsman, it is he; I know him by his look. See where my soldier shot him through the arm. He nearly missed him, but we have struck him now.

"Ah, base Châtillon, you degenerate, chief standard bearer to the Lutherans, thus, in contempt of your religion, the Duke of Guise stomps on your lifeless bulk!"

He stomped on the corpse of the Lord High Admiral: Gaspard II de Coligny, seigneur de Châtillon.

"Take the body away!" the Duke of Anjou said. "Cut off his head and hands, and send them as a present to the Pope; And, when this just revenge is finished, we will drag his corpse to Mount Faucon, and he, who while living so hated the cross, shall, being dead, be hanged on a gallows-tree in chains."

The bodies of criminals were left to rot on Mount Faucon. The Lord High Admiral's headless corpse would be hung there by the feet.

The Duke of Guise said, "Anjou, Gonzago, Retes, if you three will be as resolute as the Duke of Dumaine and me, there shall not be a Huguenot left alive to breathe in France."

The Duke of Anjou replied, "I swear by this cross, we'll not be partial, but slay as many as we can come near."

He would be impartial, and he would not be sparing of a part of the Protestants but would slay them all.

The Duke of Guise ordered, "Mountsorrell, go shoot the ordnance off so that they, who have already set their trap in the street, may know their watchword. Then toll the bell, and so let's go forward to the massacre."

Once the bell tolled, the general slaughter of Protestants would begin.

"I will, my lord," Mountsorrell said, exiting.

"And now, my lords, let's set about attentively to our business," the Duke of Guise said.

"Anjou will follow you," the Duke of Anjou said.

"And so will Dumaine," the Duke of Dumaine said.

The ordnance sounded, and then the bell tolled.

"Come, then, let's go," the Duke of Guise said.

CHAPTER 7

The Duke of Guise, along with all the others, had drawn his sword and was chasing the Protestants.

"*Tuez! Tuez! Tuez!*" the Duke of Guise shouted. "Kill! Kill! Kill! Let none escape! Murder the Huguenots!"

"Kill them!" the Duke of Anjou shouted. "Kill them!"

The Duke of Guise and the others pursued Loreine.

"Loreine, Loreine, pursue Loreine!" the Duke of Guise shouted. "Follow Loreine!"

The Duke of Guise was capable of black humor. "Follow Lorraine" was actually the rallying cry of the followers of the Cardinal of Lorraine, his brother.

They surrounded Loreine, and the Duke of Guise asked, "Sirrah, are you a preacher of these Protestant heresies?"

"Sirrah" is a term used to address a man of lower social status than the speaker.

"I am a preacher of the word of God," Loreine answered, "and you are a traitor to your soul and to God."

The Duke of Guise mocked him by saying a few words that could begin a Protestant sermon: "Dearly beloved brother."

Then he said, "Thus it is written," and stabbed Loreine.

The Duke of Anjou wanted to join in the mocking: "Wait, my lord, let me begin to sing the psalm."

"Come, drag him away and throw him in a ditch," the Duke of Guise said.

CHAPTER 8

[SCENE EIGHT]

The Catholic Mountsorrell knocked at the Protestant Seroune's door.

"Who is that who knocks there?" Seroune's wife asked.

He answered, "Mountsorrell, from the Duke of Guise."

Not knowing the danger, Seroune's wife let him in and then called, "Husband, come down; here's someone come from the Duke of Guise who wants to speak with you."

She exited to give them some privacy.

As Seroune came down, he said to himself, "To speak with me, from such a man as he?"

"Yes, yes, for this, Seroune," Mountsorrell said, showing him a dagger, "and you shall have it."

"Oh, let me pray," Seroune pleaded, "before I take my death!"

"Pray, then, quickly," Mountsorrell said.

"Oh, Christ, my Savior!" Seroune began.

"You pray to Christ, villain!" Mountsorrell said. "Why, do you dare to presume to call on Christ, without the intercession of some saint? *Sanctus Jacobus*, he's my saint; pray to him."

Sanctus Jacobus is Latin for Saint James.

"Oh, let me pray to my God!" Seroune pleaded.

"Then take this with you," Mountsorrell said, stabbing him.

"This" meant "this mortal wound."

CHAPTER 9

In his study Petrus Ramus said to himself, "What are the fearful cries that come from the river Seine and frighten poor Ramus, who is sitting and studying his book? I fear the Guisians have passed the bridge, and they mean once more to menace me."

The faction of the Duke of Guise had previously menaced Ramus, a convert to Protestantism. They had forced him to give them money.

Taleus, one of Ramus' friends, entered the study and said, "Flee, Ramus, flee, if you want to save your life!"

"Tell me, Taleus, why should I flee?" Ramus asked.

"The Guisians are close to your door, and they intend to murder us. Listen! Listen! They are coming! I'll leap out the window!"

"Dear Taleus, stay," Ramus said.

Gonzago and Retes entered the study.

"Who goes there?" Gonzago asked.

Retes said, "It is Taleus, Ramus' bedfellow."

In this society, people of the same sex often shared a bed. No sexual intimacy is implied.

"Who are you?" Gonzago asked.

"I am, as Ramus is, a Christian," Taleus said.

"Oh, let him go," Retes said. "He is a Catholic."

Gonzago said, "Come, Ramus, give us more gold, or you shall have the stab."

"But I am a scholar," Ramus said, "so how should I have gold? All that I have is only my stipend from the King, which is no sooner received than it is spent."

The Duke of Guise and the Duke of Anjou entered the study, along with the Duke of Dumaine, Mountsorrell, and some soldiers.

"Who have you there?" the Duke of Anjou asked.

"He is Ramus, the King's Professor of Logic," Retes answered.

"Stab him!" the Duke of Guise said.

"Oh, my good lord," Petrus Ramus asked, "in what has Ramus been so offensive to you?"

"Indeed, sir," the Duke of Guise replied, "in having a superficial knowledge of everything and yet never sounding anything to the depth. Wasn't it you who scoffed at the *Organon* and said it was a heap of vanities?"

The *Organon* is the name given to Aristotle's treatises on logic.

The Duke of Guise continued, "He who will be a complete and absolute dichotomist, and is expert in nothing but digests and summaries, is in your judgment thought to be a learned man."

Aristotle had criticized dichotomy, which involves dividing a whole into parts. We see dichotomy in the ancient Greek philosopher Zeno's paradox of the great warrior Achilles and a tortoise. Imagine that the two have a race, and Achilles gives the tortoise a head start. The race starts. By the time Achilles reaches the place where the tortoise started, the tortoise has moved further away. By the time Achilles reaches the place the tortoise had moved to, the tortoise will have again moved further away. And so on and so on to infinity. According to Zeno, logic says that we cannot complete an infinite series of actions, and so Achilles will never catch up to the tortoise.

Another example is Zeno's paradox that is actually called the Dichotomy Paradox. Imagine that Homer wishes to walk to the end of a path. First, he has to walk halfway there. Then he has to walk half of the distance remaining. Then he has to walk half of the distance that is still remaining. And so on and so on to infinity. According to Zeno, logic says that we cannot complete an infinite series of actions, and so Homer will never reach the end of the path.

Aristotle had also criticized another form of dichotomy, which is a form of logical classification that involves dividing a class into two subclasses. For example, students can be divided into those who study philosophy and those who don't. These subclasses can be further divided.

Aristotle felt that often dichotomy doesn't work because the same thing can be placed in different classes or subclasses. For example, a biracial person can be placed in two classes of races.

Petrus Ramus had in fact severely criticized Aristotle's thought, which was greatly respected in the Middle Ages.

The Duke of Guise continued, "And the man you consider learned, indeed, must go and teach in Germany."

Ramus himself had taught at the University of Heidelberg.

The Duke of Guise continued, "The man you consider learned must take exception to doctors' axioms and actions, and must take exception to *ipse dixi* with this quiddity: *Argumentum testimonii est inartificiale.*"

"*Ipse dixi*" is Latin for "I have spoken." Roughly, it means that something is true because the speaker said it. It is an assertion that is made without supporting evidence: "That's just how things are."

A quiddity is a subtlety: a little, picky point.

In this context, the meaning of "*Argumentum testimonii est inartificiale*" is basically "Argument based on the authority of the person making the argument is not of its own nature conclusive." In other words, it takes more than that authority to determine whether something is true: Even an expert can be wrong.

The Duke of Guise continued, "To contradict which, I say, Ramus shall die."

In other words, the Duke of Guise was saying this: Ramus shall die. *Ipse dixi.* It is true because I have said it. I shall prove that the statement is true by making sure that Ramus dies.

The Duke of Guise continued, "How do you answer that? Your *nego argumentum* cannot serve."

"*Nego argumentum*" is Latin for "I deny [the validity of] the argument."

The Duke of Guise ordered, "Sirrah, kill him!"

Ramus said, "Oh, my good lord, let me but speak a word!"

"Well, speak," the Duke of Anjou said.

"Not for my life do I desire this pause," Ramus said, "but in my last hour I desire to clear myself of suspicion of guilt, in that I know the things that I have written, which, as I hear, one Jacob Scheckius — one of my major philosophical opponents — takes those things ill, because my places, being but three, contain all his."

Jacob Scheckius is also known as Jakob Schegk. He was a German Aristotelian philosopher who lived from 1511 to 1587.

The word "places" comes from the Latin word "*loci*." Sometimes "*loci*" is translated as "topics." One of Aristotle's six works on logic collected in the *Organon* was titled *Topics*. This work concerned topical logic and topical argumentation. In it, Aristotle developed heuristics — approaches and techniques — for developing arguments that started from positions (places, topics, places, *loci*) that had already been thought about and developed. This is useful in rhetoric.

Ramus continued, "I knew Aristotle's *Organon* to be confused, and I reduced it into better form."

To "reduce" something is to give it a certain form. Ramus had earlier been accused of being "expert in nothing but digests and summaries." His excuse was that he was simply taking unclear thought and making it clear.

Ramus continued, "And I will say this for Aristotle: He who despises Aristotle can never be good in logic or philosophy. And I say that because of the blockheaded doctors and students at the Sorbonne — the faculty of theology in the University of Paris — who attribute as much to their works as to the service of the eternal God."

According to the *Oxford English Dictionary*, "attribute as much" means "to ascribe great importance to, to hold in high estimation."

In 1543, Ramus had published his book *Dialectical Institutions*, which the doctors at the Sorbonne had suppressed because it criticized Aristotle.

Of course, Ramus had long been critical of Aristotle. According to his biographer Johannes Thomas Freigius, in 1536 Ramus defended in public the thesis "*quaecumque ab Aristotele dicta essent, commentitia esse.*"

Walter J. Ong, S.J., analyzed this Latin statement in his book *Ramus, Method, and the Decay of Dialogue: From the Art of Discourse to the Art of Reason* (1958: 46-47) and paraphrases it in this way:

"All the things that Aristotle has said are inconsistent because they are poorly systematized and can be called to mind only by the use of arbitrary mnemonic devices."

The Duke of Guise said, "Why do you allow that peasant to declaim? Stab him, I say, and send him to his friends in hell."

"Never was there another collier's son so full of pride," the Duke of Anjou said.

Ramus was humbly born; his father was a charcoal-burner.

The Duke of Anjou killed Ramus.

The Duke of Guise said, "My Lord of Anjou, there are a hundred Protestants whom we have chased into the river Seine. They swim about, and so preserve their lives. What may we do? I fear that they will live."

"Go place some men upon the bridge, with bows and arrows, to shoot at the Protestants they see, and sink them in the river as they swim," the Duke of Dumaine said.

"That is good advice, Duke of Dumaine," the Duke of Guise said. "Go and see to it immediately."

The Duke of Dumaine exited.

The Duke of Guise then said, "And in the meantime, my lord, could we devise a way to get those schoolteachers away from the King of Navarre? They are tutors to him and the Prince of Condé."

"As for that, leave it to me," the Duke of Anjou said.

They went to the place where the King of Navarre and the Prince of Condé were staying with their schoolteachers.

The Duke of Anjou said to the Duke of Guise, "Kinsman, stay here, and when you see me inside, then follow closely behind me."

The Duke of Anjou knocked. The King of Navarre, the Prince of Condé, and their schoolteachers came outside.

The Duke of Anjou asked, "How are you now, my lords? How do you fare?"

"My lord, they say that all the Protestants are massacred," the King of Navarre said.

"Yes, so they are," the Duke of Anjou said, "but yet, what can be done? I have done what I could to bring this turmoil under control."

His way of doing that was killing Protestants until no Protestants were left to kill.

"But yet, my lord, the report is that you were one of those who made this massacre," the King of Navarre said.

"Who? I?" the Duke of Anjou said. "You are deceived," he lied. "I rose out of bed just now."

The Duke of Guise, with Gonzago, Retes, Mountsorrell, and some soldiers came forward.

The Duke of Guise ordered, "Murder the Huguenots! Take those schoolteachers away from here!"

"You traitor, Duke of Guise, lay off your bloody hands!" the King of Navarre said.

They fought, and then they broke apart.

The Prince of Condé said to the King of Navarre, "Come, let us go tell King Charles IX."

The two men broke away and fled, but the schoolteachers were physically prevented from leaving.

The Duke of Guise said, "Come, sirs, I'll whip you to death with my poniard's point."

The Duke of Guise was capable of black humor. Part of a schoolteacher's job at the time was to whip misbehaving schoolboys. A poniard is a dagger.

He killed the two schoolteachers with his dagger.

The Duke of Anjou ordered, "Away with them both!"

He and some soldiers carrying the bodies exited.

The Duke of Guise said, "And now, sirs, for this night let our fury cease. Yet we do not wish that the massacre shall end.

"Gonzago, ride posthaste to Orleans. Retes, you ride posthaste to Dieppe. Mountsorrell, you ride posthaste to Rouen. Spare no one whom you suspect of heresy."

They exited.

The Duke of Guise continued, "And now stop the ringing of that bell, that to the devil's matins rings."

"Matins" is a prayer service held in the morning. The St. Bartholomew's Day Massacre had occurred in the morning. The massacre would not stop here and now, but would spread to other cities in France. The killing of Protestants by Catholics would continue for over two months.

The Duke of Guise ordered, "Now every man put off his light helmet, and so steal covertly to his bed."

CHAPTER 10

The Duke of Anjou talked with two Lords of Poland.

"My Lords of Poland, I must necessarily confess that the offer of your Prince Electors for me to be King of Poland is far beyond the reach of my deserts. For Poland is, as I have been informed, a country of martial people, worthy of such a King as has sufficient counsel in himself to lighten doubts, and frustrate cunning foes. Such a King, whom practice long has taught to please himself with the management of the wars, the greatest wars within our Christian boundaries — I mean our wars against the Muscovites, who are led by Ivan the Terrible, and on the other side against the Turk. They are both rich princes, and mighty emperors.

"Yet, by my brother Charles IX, our King of France, and by his grace's council, it is thought that, if I undertake to wear the crown of Poland, it may prejudice their hope of my inheritance of the crown of France once my brother dies. For, if the Almighty takes my brother away from here, by due descent the regal seat is mine.

"With Poland, therefore, I must make this covenant: If, by the death of Charles IX, the diadem of France would be cast on me, then with your permission, I may retire to my native home of France.

"If your commission serves to warrant this, I thankfully shall undertake the charge of you and yours, and carefully maintain the wealth and safety of your kingdom's right."

The first Polish lord said, "All this, and more, your highness shall command for Poland's crown and kingly diadem."

"Then, come, my lords, let's go," the Duke of Anjou said.

The Duke of Anjou reigned as King of Poland from 16 May 1573 to 12 May 1575.

In fact, the Duke of Anjou did succeed Charles XI as King of France, and he became known as King Henry III of France.

He reigned as King Henry III of France from 30 May 1574 to 2 August 1589.

33

CHAPTER 11

Two soldiers who were carrying the Lord High Admiral's body were in the mood for black humor. They knew that their orders were to hang the body from a gallows-tree, but they joked about other ways to dispose of the body.

The first soldier said, "Now, sirrah, what shall we do with the Lord High Admiral?"

"Why, let us burn him for a heretic," the second soldier said.

"Oh, no, his body will infect the fire, and the fire will infect the air, and we will breathe the air and so we shall be poisoned with him."

This society believed that noxious odors could transmit disease.

"What shall we do, then?" the second soldier asked.

"Let's throw him into the river."

"Oh, it will corrupt the water, and the water will corrupt the fish, and we ourselves will be corrupted by the fish, when we eat them."

"Then let's throw him into the ditch," the first soldier said.

"No, no. To decide all doubts, take my advice: Let's hang him here upon this gallows-tree."

"Agreed."

They hung the headless body by the feet on the gallows-tree and exited.

The Duke of Guise, Catherine the Queen-Mother, and the Cardinal of Lorraine came to see the body. Some attendants accompanied them.

"Now, madam," the Duke of Guise asked, "how do you like our lusty Admiral?"

Meanings of "lusty" include "strong," "brave," and "healthy."

"Believe me, Duke of Guise, he becomes the place so well that I could have wished him there long before this," Catherine the Queen-Mother said. "But come, let's walk a little ways off because the air's not very sweet."

"No, it is not, by my faith, madam," the Duke of Guise said.

He ordered, "Sirs, take him away, and throw him in some ditch."

Some attendants carried away the Lord High Admiral's dead body.

The Duke of Guise then said, "And now, madam, I understand that there are a hundred and more Huguenots who in the woods hold their 'synagogue,' and daily meet about this time of day, and thither I will go to put them to the sword."

"Do so, sweet Guise," Catherine the Queen-Mother said. "Let us not delay, for if these stragglers regroup and gather strength again and disperse throughout the realm of France, it will be hard for us to work their deaths. Leave now; don't delay, sweet Guise."

"Madam, I go as whirlwinds rage before a storm," the Duke of Guise replied.

He exited.

Using the royal plural, Catherine the Queen-Mother said, "My Lord Cardinal of Lorraine, have you noticed recently how Charles our son begins to lament the recent night's work that my Lord of Guise made in Paris amongst the Huguenots? Now he regrets the massacre."

"Madam, I have heard him solemnly vow, along with the rebellious King of Navarre, to revenge their deaths upon us all," the Cardinal of Lorraine replied.

"Yes, but, my lord, leave that to me, for Catherine — I — must have her will in France," she said. "As I do live, so surely shall he die, and the Duke of Anjou then shall wear the diadem as King Henry III of France.

"And, if he should grudge or cross his mother's will, I'll disinherit him and all the rest. For I'll rule France, but they shall wear the crown, and, if they storm and complain, I then may pull them down and overthrow them.

"Come, my lord, let us go."

CHAPTER 12

Five or six Protestants holding books knelt together in a wood to worship God.

The Duke of Guise and some other armed men crept toward them.

When they were close to the worshippers, the Duke of Guise shouted, "Down with the Huguenots! Murder them!"

The first Protestant pleaded, "Oh, Monsieur de Guise, just hear me speak!"

"No, villain," the Duke of Guise replied. "That tongue of yours that has blasphemed the holy Church of Rome shall drive no complaints and lamentations into the Guise's ears to make the justice of my heart relent."

He shouted, "*Tuez! Tuez! Tuez!* Kill! Kill! Kill! Let none escape!"

The armed men killed the Protestants.

The Duke of Guise then ordered, "Drag their bodies away."

CHAPTER 13

[SCENE THIRTEEN]

Very ill, King Charles IX of France stood with the King of Navarre and the Duke of Epernoun supporting him. Catherine the Queen-Mother and the Cardinal of Lorraine walked over to them.

"Oh, let me stay, and rest me here a while," King Charles IX of France said. "An agonizing pain has seized upon my heart, a sudden pang, the messenger of death."

"Oh, don't say that," Catherine the Queen-Mother said. "You are killing your mother's heart."

"I must say that," King Charles IX said. "The pain forces me to complain."

"Comfort yourself, my lord," the King of Navarre said, "and have no doubt that God will surely restore you to your health."

"Oh, no, my loving brother of Navarre!" King Charles IX said. "I have deserved a scourge, I must confess. Yet there is patience of another sort than to misdo the welfare of their King. May God grant that my nearest friends may prove no worse!"

Because of guilt about the massacre, King Charles IX of France believed that he deserved a scourge from God. Humans, however, could take that responsibility on themselves by harming their King — for example, by poisoning him. The alternative, of course, was simply to be calm and patient and not harm their King — instead, wait and let God be the scourge. King Charles IX hoped that his friends would do no worse than to be calm and patient.

Charles IX said, "Oh, hold me up, my sight begins to fail, my muscles shrink, my brains turn upside down, my heart breaks. I faint and die."

He died in their arms.

His mother, Catherine, said, "Are you dead, sweet son? Speak to your mother! Oh, no, his soul has fled from out his breast, and he neither hears nor sees us and what we do."

She immediately turned to political business:

"My lords, what remains now to be done except that we immediately dispatch ambassadors to Poland, to call the Duke of Anjou — soon to be King Henry III of France — back again, so he can wear his brother's crown and dignity.

"Epernoun, go and see that it immediately is done, and tell him to come without delay to us."

"Madam, I will," the Duke of Epernoun said, and then he exited.

Catherine the Queen-Mother then said, "And now, my lords, after these funeral rites are done, we will, with all the speed we can, provide arrangements for Henry's coronation after he comes from Poland.

"Come, let us take Charles IX's body away."

Everyone exited except the King of Navarre and his friend Pleshé.

"And now, Pleshé, while these quarrels between the Catholics and Protestants continue, they give me a suitable opportunity to steal away from France, and hurry to my home in Navarre.

"There's no safety in the French realm for me, and now that the Duke of Anjou is called from Poland to become King Henry III, it is my due, by just succession.

"And therefore, as speedily as I can perform, I'll muster up an army secretly, for fear that the Duke of Guise, joined with the King of Spain, might seek to cross me in some enterprise.

"But God, Who always defends the right, will show His mercy, and preserve us still."

The King of Navarre was thinking ahead. If King Henry III were to die, then he could become King of France. (Actually, if both King Henry III and his younger brother, the Duke of Alençon, were to die, then the King of Navarre would become King of France.) To eventually become King of France, however, the King of Navarre would have to stay alive, something that the Duke of Guise opposed. Therefore, the King of Navarre would quickly and secretly start to raise an army.

Pleshé replied, "The virtues of our true religion cannot but march with many more graces. That army shall discomfort all your foes, and in the end, that army shall crown you in Pamplona in spite of Spain and all the popish power that holds it from your highness wrongfully. Your majesty is Pamplona's rightful lord and sovereign."

Pamplona was the capital of Navarre, but Spain, a Catholic country, possessed and controlled Pamplona.

The King of Navarre replied, "Pleshé, that is the truth, and may God so prosper me in everything, as I intend to labor for the truth and for the true profession of His holy word.

"Come, Pleshé, let's leave while the time for leaving is good."

CHAPTER 14

[SCENE FOURTEEN]

On 13 February 1575, King Henry III of France stood, wearing a crown. Also present were Catherine the Queen-Mother, the Cardinal of Lorraine, the Duke of Guise, the King's minions (the Duke of Joyeux and Mugeroun), with others, including attendants, and a cutpurse (a thief).

King Henry III had just been crowned and was now going to the palace.

Trumpets sounded, and a crowd of people all cried, "*Vive le roi!*" ("May the King live!" or "[Long] live the King!") three times.

"Welcome home from Poland, Henry, once again," Catherine the Queen-Mother said. "Welcome to France, your father's royal seat. Here you have a country void of fears, a warlike people to maintain your right, a watchful and vigilant senate for ordaining laws, a loving mother to preserve your state, and all things else that a King may wish for — all this, and more, has Henry III with his crown."

"And long may King Henry III enjoy all this, and more!" the Cardinal of Lorraine said.

The members of the crowd shouted, "*Vive le roi! Vive le roi!*"

Trumpets sounded.

"Thanks to you all," King Henry III said. "May the Guider of all crowns — God — grant that our deeds may well deserve your loves. And so they shall, if fortune carries out my will and yields your thoughts to the height of my deserts."

He meant that his deeds would in fact deserve the love and respect of the people if two things were to happen:

1) Lady Fortune would carry out his will to do deeds worthy of the love and respect of the people, and

2) Lady Fortune would make the thoughts of the people love and respect the King's deeds — which would be worthy because of #1 — to the degree that they deserved.

He then said to the Duke of Joyeux and Mugeroun, "What say our minions?"

The word "minion" can mean "favorite," but it can also mean "lover."

King Henry III continued, "Do my minions think that Henry's heart will not harbor both love and majesty? Put off that fear because love and majesty are already joined in my heart. No person, place, time, or circumstance shall slacken my love's affection from its natural inclination. As you now are, so shall you still remain, persist, and continue to be irremovable from the favors of your King."

He meant either that they would continue to be his favorites or continue to be his male lovers, or both.

Mugeroun replied, "We know that noble minds do not change their thoughts because of the wearing of a crown. We know that because your grace has worn the diadem of Poland, before you were invested in the crown of France."

"I tell you, Mugeroun, we will be friends, and fellows, too, whatever storms arise," King Henry III said.

For a person to be a "fellow" with a King, the two must have a very close relationship.

Mugeroun said, "Then may it please your majesty to give me permission to punish those who profane this holy feast."

The cutpurse had been cutting off the gold buttons on Mugeroun's cloak, and now Mugeroun cut off an ear of the cutpurse.

King Henry III asked, "What do you mean by that?"

"Oh, lord, my ear!" the cutpurse cried.

"Come, sir, give me my gold buttons back, and here's your ear," Mugeroun said.

Mugeroun grabbed the gold buttons and gave the cutpurse the ear.

"Sirrah, take him away," the Duke of Guise ordered an attendant.

"Hands off, good fellow," King Henry III said to the attendant. "I will be his bail for this offense."

He then said to the cutpurse, "Go, sirrah, work no more until this our coronation day is past."

The cutpurse exited.

King Henry III then said, "And now, our solemn rites of coronation done, what now remains but to feast for a while, and spend some days enjoying games of barriers, tourney, tilt, and such entertainments as are fitting for the court?"

Barriers were a martial exercise whose nature appears to have been varied, but which sometimes involved men fighting with short swords. Tourneys were tournaments and involved two groups of fighters. Tilts were combats between two men on horseback who were armed with spears or lances.

"Let's go, my lords," King Henry III said. "Our dinner waits for us."

Everyone exited except Catherine the Queen-Mother and the Cardinal of Lorraine.

"My Lord Cardinal of Lorraine, tell me, how does your grace like my son's pleasantness? His mind, you see, runs on his minions, and all his heaven is to delight himself."

She added, "And, while he sleeps securely and overconfidently thus in ease, your brother the Duke of Guise and we may now make provisions to plant and establish ourselves with such authority as not a man may live without our permissions. Then shall the Catholic faith of Rome flourish in France, and none deny the same."

The Cardinal of Lorraine replied, "Madam, as in secrecy I was told, my brother the Duke of Guise has gathered an army of men for the purpose, he says, of killing the Puritans, but it is the House of Bourbon that he means."

The King of Navarre was a member of the House — the Family — of Bourbon. His father was Antoine de Bourbon: King Antoine of Navarre.

"Now, madam," the Cardinal of Lorraine continued, "you must insinuate ideas and tell King Henry III this is for his country's good and the common profit of religion.

"Tush, man, let me alone with him," Catherine the Queen-Mother said, "and I will work the way to bring this thing to pass. And, if he refuses to do what I tell him to do, I'll dispatch him and send him to his brother in Paradise immediately, and then shall Monsieur wear the diadem."

By "Monsieur," she meant the Duke of Alençon, King Henry III's younger brother and the next in line to the throne of France.

She continued, "Tush, all shall die unless I have my will, for, while she lives, Catherine will be Queen.

"Come, my lord, let us go seek the Duke of Guise and then make our final decisions about this enterprise."

CHAPTER 15

The Duchess of Guise was in her private chamber with her maid.

"Go fetch me pen and ink —" the Duchess of Guise ordered.

"I will, madam," the maid said and then exited.

"— so that I may write to my dearest lord," the Duchess of Guise said to herself. "Sweet Mugeroun, it is he who has my heart, and the Duke of Guise usurps it because I am his wife.

"I would love to find some means to speak with Mugeroun, but I cannot, and therefore I am forced to write him in order that he may come and meet me in some place where we may each enjoy the other's sight."

The maid returned with ink and paper.

The Duchess of Guise ordered, "So, set it down, and leave me to myself."

The maid placed ink and paper on the table and then exited.

As the Duchess of Guise wrote, she said to herself, "Oh, I wish to God that this quill that I write with here had lately been plucked from the fair god of love Cupid's wing, so that it might print these lines within his heart!"

The Duke of Guise entered her private chamber.

"All alone, my love?" he said. "And writing, too? Please, tell me to whom you are writing."

"To such a woman, my lord, who when she reads my lines, will laugh, I am afraid, at their 'good array,'" his wife replied.

"Array" means "arrangement." She was speaking ironically, and she meant that her letter would be laughed at because the words were improperly arranged — in other words, the letter would be laughed at because it was badly written.

"Please, let me see it," the Duke of Guise said.

"Oh, no, my lord," his wife said. "Only a woman must partake of the secrets of my heart."

"But, madam, I must see your letter," the Duke of Guise insisted.

He forcibly took it from her and read it.

Then he said, "Are these your secrets that no man must know!"

"Oh, pardon me, my lord!" his wife said.

"You disloyal, faithless, unjust, false, and perjured woman, what lines are these?" the Duke of Guise said. "Am I grown old, or is your lust grown young? Am I now too old for you?

"Or has my love been so obscured in you, that others need to comment on my text?"

Scholars of the Middle Ages often commented on obscure texts.

He continued, "Is all my love forgotten, which held you dear? Is that true, you who are dearer than the apple of my eye? Is Guise's glory only a cloudy mist in the sight and judgment of your lustful eye?

"*Mort dieu!* [God's death!] I swear by the death of God that were it not for the fruit within your womb, on whose increase I set some longing hope, this wrathful hand would strike you to the heart."

His wife was pregnant.

The Duke of Guise continued, "Hence, strumpet, hide your head for shame, and flee from my presence, if you want to live!"

His wife the Duchess exited.

Alone, the Duke of Guise said to himself, "Oh, wicked sex, perjured and unjust, now do I see that from the very first her eyes and looks sowed seeds of perjury."

She had committed perjury because during the wedding ceremony she had vowed to be faithful to him, but her letter showed that at least in her heart she was not.

He continued, "But that villain — Mugeroun — to whom these lines were supposed to go, shall buy her love even with his dearest blood."

CHAPTER 16

[SCENE SIXTEEN]

The King of Navarre and his friends Pleshé and Bartus met together. The King's train of attendants, as well as drummers and trumpeters, was present.

The King of Navarre said, "My lords, in a just and right quarrel we undertake to manage these our wars against the proud disturbers of the faith — I mean the Duke of Guise, the Pope, and the King of Spain — who set themselves to tread us under foot, and rend our true Protestant religion from this land.

"You, of course, know that our objective in fighting is no more than to ward off their strange, extreme religious inventions, which they will subject us to with sword and fire. If they are victorious, they will either kill us or force us to convert to Catholicism.

"Therefore, we must with resolute minds resolve to fight in honor of our God and our country's good.

"Spain is the council chamber of the Pope, for Spain is the place where he makes peace and war. And the Duke of Guise in support of the King of Spain has now incensed and incited King Henry III of France to send his army to meet us in the field."

Bartus said, "Then in this bloody brunt they may behold the sole endeavor of your princely care, which is to plant the true succession of the faith, in spite of the King of Spain and all his heresies."

The King of Navarre said, "The power of Vengeance now encamps itself upon the haughty mountains of my breast, which plays with Vengeance's gory colors of revenge. I regard Vengeance and her colors as metaphorical leaves of dark green that change their color to blood-red when the winter approaches — with that change of color to blood-red I shall vaunt as victor in revenge. In other words, my metaphorical leaves have been dark-green and with the approach of this war they are changing to blood-red; I have been a man of peace, but soon I will be a man of war and vengeance."

A messenger entered.

"What is it, sirrah?" the King of Navarre asked. "What news do you bring?"

"My lord, our scouts inform us that a mighty army is speedily coming from France. That army is already mustered in the land, and it intends to meet your highness in the field."

"In God's name, let them come!" the King of Navarre said. "This is the work of the Duke of Guise, who has incensed King Henry III of France to levy arms and make these civil wars. But can you tell me who is their general?"

"Not yet, my lord," the messenger answered, "because they are waiting for their general to be appointed. But, as rumor has it, the Duke of Joyeux has mightily requested that King Henry III of England make him the army's general."

"His being named general will not countervail — be an equal return for — his pains, I hope," the King of Navarre said.

In other words, the King of Navarre hoped that if the Duke of Joyeux were made general, he would fare badly on the battlefield.

The King of Navarre continued, "I wish the Duke of Guise might have come as general instead, but he hides himself within his drowsy couch, and makes his footstool out of overconfidence in his security. As long as he is safe, he doesn't care what becomes of his King or his country; no, he doesn't care about either of them.

"But come, my lords, let us go now with speed and place ourselves in order for the fight."

CHAPTER 17

King Henry III of France, the Duke of Guise, the Duke of Epernoun, and the Duke of Joyeux talked together.

King Henry III of France said, "My sweet Joyeux, I make you the general of all my army, which is now ready to march against the rebellious King of Navarre. You requested to be made general, and because of that I allow your leaving to lead the army, although my love for you can only with great difficulty allow it because I am always aware of the danger to your life that leading an army into battle entails."

"I give thanks to your majesty, and so I take my leave," the Duke of Joyeux replied.

He added, "Farewell to my lord Guise and to Epernoun."

The Duke of Guise said, "I wish health and give a hearty farewell to my lord Joyeux."

The Duke of Joyeux exited.

King Henry III said, "Kinsman of Guise, you and your wife both salute our lovely minions very lovingly."

King Henry III, who was aware of the letter that the Duke of Guise's wife had written to Mugeroun, used his forefingers to make horns on his head as he looked at the Duke of Guise. This was an insult. Cuckolds, aka men with unfaithful wives, were said to have invisible horns growing on their foreheads.

He added, "Do you remember the letter, gentle sir, that your wife wrote to my dear minion, who is her chosen friend?"

By "friend," he meant "lover."

"What is this, my lord!" the Duke of Guise, a very proud man, said. "Truly, by my faith, what you are saying is more than there is need for. Am I thus to be mocked at and scorned? This is more than is fitting for a King or an Emperor. And, to be sure, if all the proudest Kings in Christendom should bear me such derision, they would know how I scorned them and their mocking actions and speeches.

"I love your minions! Dote on them yourself! I know no one else who does; all others regard them as disgraceful. And here, I swear by all the saints in heaven that that villain for whom I bear this deep disgrace — even for your words that have incensed and angered me so — shall buy that strumpet's favor with his blood, whether or not he has dishonored me.

"*Par la mort de Dieu, il mourra!* I swear by the death of God that he shall die!"

The Duke of Guise exited.

King Henry III of France said, "Believe me, this jest bites sore. It went much worse than I expected."

"My lord, it is a good idea to make the Duke of Guise and Mugeroun friends, for the Duke of Guise's oaths are seldom made in vain," the Duke of Epernoun said.

Mugeroun entered the room.

"How are you now, Mugeroun?" King Henry III asked. "Didn't you meet the Duke of Guise at the door?"

"No, my lord," Mugeroun answered. "Why do you ask?"

"Indeed," King Henry III said, "if you had met him at the door, you might have gotten stabbed, for he has solemnly sworn to kill you."

"I may be stabbed, and still live until he is dead," Mugeroun said.

His words had more than one meaning: 1) The Duke of Guise could stab him, and yet he could kill the Duke of Guise before dying, and 2) The Duke of Guise is not the man who will kill him.

In addition, the sentence can be interpreted bawdily. In this culture, the phrase "to die" can mean "to have an orgasm." The stabbing could be a homosexual "stabbing," aka sodomy.

"But why does he bear me such deadly hate?" Mugeroun asked.

King Henry III answered, "Because his wife bears you such kindly love."

The word "bear" can mean to "bear Mugeroun's weight while having sex with him."

"If that is all, the next time that I meet her, I'll make her shake off love with her heels," Mugeroun said.

Heels can be held high and shook in the act of making love. He would make her repudiate her love for him and repudiate shaking her heels while with him. Or, possibly, he would make her repudiate her love for him by having rough sex with her and making her heels shake.

He then asked, "But which way has the Duke of Guise gone? I'll go make a walk on purpose from the court to meet him."

He exited.

King Henry III said, "I don't like this. Come, Epernoun, let us go seek the Duke of Guise, and make him and Mugeroun friends."

CHAPTER 18

On 20 October 1587, the Protestant army led by King Henry of Navarre won a decisive victory against the Catholic army led by the Duke of Joyeux, who was slain in the Battle of Coutras.

The King of Navarre said, "The Duke of Joyeux is slain, and all his army has been dispersed, and we are graced with wreaths of victory. Thus God, we see, always guides the right side in order to make His glory great upon the earth."

His friend Bartus said, "I hope that the terror to the French of this happy Huguenot victory will make King Henry III of France abandon his hate, and either never manage an army any more, or else employ the army's soldiers in some better cause."

"How many noblemen have lost their lives in the prosecution of these cruel arms and savage war is a matter of grief and ruth, and almost death, to call to mind," the King of Navarre said. "But we know God will always put down them who lift themselves against the perfect truth.

"I'll maintain the perfect truth as long as my life does last, and I will join my force with Queen Elizabeth of England to beat the papal monarch from our lands and keep those Catholic relics from our country's coasts and borders.

"Come, my lords; now that this storm is over and past, let us go away with triumph to our tents."

CHAPTER 19

[SCENE NINETEEN]

A soldier, holding a musket and waiting in ambush to kill Mugeroun in behalf of the Duke of Guise, talked to himself. Much of what he said had a bawdy double meaning:

"Now, sir, I turn to you who dares make a Duke a cuckold, and use a counterfeit key to enter his privy chamber. Although you take out none but your own treasure, yet you put in that which displeases him, and fill up his room that he should occupy."

The word "occupy" had a then-current sexual meaning.

"Fill up his room" means "Fills the Duke of Guise's wife's vagina with semen."

The soldier continued:

"Herein, sir, you forestall the market."

One way to forestall the market is to buy up the goods ahead of time. It is a way to manipulate and change market prices.

The soldier continued:

"And, herein, sir, you set up your standing where you should not."

The soldier was using the image of a merchant setting up a stall in a place that should be occupied by a different merchant's stall. With this image, the soldier is accusing Mugeroun of setting up a standing, aka an erection, in a forbidden place, aka the Duke of Guise's wife's vagina.

The soldier continued:

"But you will say you leave him room enough besides. That's no answer: He's to have the choice of his own free land — if it be not too free, there's the question.

"Now for where he is your landlord, you take upon you to be his, and will needs enter what is his by default.

"What though you were once in possession, yet coming upon you once unawares, he frayed you out again; therefore, your entry is mere intrusion. This is against the law, sir."

Apparently, the Duke of Guise had caught his wife and Mugeroun in the act of love-making, and he had then "frayed" — frightened and fought — Mugeroun and driven him out of the Duchess of Guise's vagina.

The soldier continued:

"And although I haven't come to keep possession, as I wish I might, yet I come to keep you out, sir — which I will, if this gear hold."

The soldier meant that he would keep Mugeroun out of the Duke of Guise's wife's vagina if this "gear" — this plan — works and if this "gear" — this musket — works.

Mugeroun appeared, walking nearby.

The soldier said, "What, have you come so soon? You are welcome, sir! Have at you, sir!"

"Have at you" is an exclamation indicating that the speaker is about to attack someone.

The soldier shot at Mugeroun, giving him a mortal wound.

"Traitorous Guise!" Mugeroun said, falling to the ground. "Ah, you have murdered me."

He died.

The Duke of Guise arrived and said to the soldier, "Wait, brave soldier!"

He gave the soldier some money and said, "Take this and flee."

The soldier took the money and exited.

The Duke of Guise said to Mugeroun's corpse, "Thus fall, you imperfect exhalation that our great son of France could not effect — you fiery meteor in the firmament. Lie there, King Henry III's delight and Guise's scorn!"

To the Duke of Guise, Mugeroun was like a malignant heavenly omen. He was also a favorite of King Henry III, a favorite whom the King could not protect.

The Duke of Guise wanted Mugeroun dead, something that King Henry III did not want. The King was unable to effect — accomplish — his intention of keeping Mugeroun safe.

By killing Mugeroun, the Duke of Guise was getting rid of a malignant omen. This is something that King Henry III was unable to effect, to accomplish — because the King wanted Mugeroun alive.

The Duke of Guise then said, "Revenge this death, Henry III, if you wish to or dare to. I did it only to spite you. Foolishly have you incensed the Guise's soul that of itself was already hot enough to inflict your just digestion with the most extreme shame.

"The army I have gathered now shall aim at your end, your extirpation; and when you think I have forgotten this, and when you most have faith in my faith, then I will awaken you from your foolish dream and let you see that you yourself are my prisoner."

The Duke of Guise carried away Mugeroun's corpse.

CHAPTER 20

King Henry III of France, the Duke of Epernoun, and the Duke of Guise met.

King Henry III said, "My Lord of Guise, we understand that you have gathered an army of men. What your intention is we cannot learn up to now, but we presume it is not for our good."

"Why, I am no traitor to the crown of France," the Duke of Guise said. "What I have done, it is for the gospel's sake."

"No, it is for the Pope's sake, and for your own benefit," the Duke of Epernoun said. "What peer in France, but you, ambitious Guise, dare to be in arms without the King's consent? I charge you with treason in this matter."

"Ah, base Epernoun!" the Duke of Guise said. "If his highness were not here, you would perceive that the Duke of Guise is angry."

"Be patient, Guise, and don't threaten Epernoun, lest you perceive that the King of France is angry," King Henry III said.

"Why, I am a prince of the Valois' line, and therefore I am an enemy to the Bourbonites," the Duke of Guise said.

Actually, the Duke of Guise was a member of the House of Lorraine; the House of Valois was the royal family. He, however, was claiming to be related to King Henry III and the House of Valois because his cousin Mary Queen of Scots had married Francis II, Henry III's older brother. King Francis II of France ruled from 10 July 1559 to 5 December 1560 and died at age sixteen.

The Duke of Guise continued, "I am a juror in and have sworn allegiance to the Holy League, and I am therefore hated by the Protestants."

The Holy League was an organization designed to promote Catholicism; it is sometimes called the Catholic League.

He continued, "What should I do but stand upon my guard and be vigilant? And, being able, I'll keep an army in my pay."

"You able to maintain an army in pay!" the Duke of Epernoun said. "You who live by foreign monetary maintenance! The Pope and the King of Spain are your good friends; all France knows how poor a Duke you are if not for that."

"Yes, those are they who feed him with their gold," King Henry III of France said, "to countermand and oppose our will, and check and repress our friends."

The Duke of Guise replied, "My lord, to speak more plainly, this is how it is: Being animated and inspired by religious zeal, I mean to muster all the power I can to overthrow those factious, sectarian Puritans.

"Know that before I shall lack anything the Pope will sell his triple crown, yes, and the Catholic Philip, King of Spain, will cause his Indians to rip into the golden bowels of America and send gold to support me.

"The King of Navarre, who cloaks those factious and sectarian Puritans underneath his wings, shall feel the House of Lorraine is his foe.

"Your highness needs not fear my army's force and power. It is for your safety, and for your enemies' ruin."

King Henry III said sarcastically, "Guise, wear our crown, and be King of France and, as Dictator, make either war or peace, while I cry, '*Placet!* — It pleases me!' — like a Senator!"

The ancient Romans would in times of crisis elect a dictator with very much power, including power that normally belonged to the Senate, to handle the crisis. Roman Senators voted "yes" by saying, "*Placet!* — It pleases me!"

King Henry III continued, "I cannot endure your haughty, arrogant insolence. Dismiss your camp of soldiers, or else by our edict you will find yourself proclaimed a traitor throughout France."

The Duke of Guise thought, *The choice is hard; I must lie to the King.*

He said out loud, "My lord, in token of my true humility, and innocent intentions to your majesty, I kiss your grace's hand, and take my leave, intending to speedily dislodge my camp of soldiers."

King Henry III replied, "Then farewell, Duke of Guise. The King and you are friends."

The Duke of Guise exited.

The Duke of Epernoun said, "But don't trust him, my lord, for if your highness had seen with what pomp he entered Paris and how the citizens with gifts and shows entertained him, and promised to be at his command — indeed, they weren't afraid to say in the streets that the Duke of Guise dared to stand in arms against the King — you — because you have not done what his holiness the Pope wants you to do."

King Henry III had made some overtures of religious tolerance regarding the Protestants. The Edict of Beaulieu, which was promulgated on 6 May 1576, gave the Huguenots the right of public worship.

"Did they of Paris entertain him so?" King Henry III said. "Then he intends immediate treason to our state. Well, leave it to me."

He summoned a servant: "Who's within there?"

An attendant entered, carrying a document, pen, and ink. The attendant was well prepared; a superior attendant knows what the master wants before the master asks for it.

King Henry III ordered, "Make a document of discharge of all my council immediately, and I'll sign my name and seal it immediately. That document will dismiss all the members of my council. My head shall be my council; they are false."

He added, "Epernoun, I will be ruled by you. I will listen to your advice and be guided by it."

The Duke of Epernoun immediately gave the King some advice:

"My lord, I think, for the safety of your royal person, it would be good if the Duke of Guise were made away with, and in such a way that your grace is free from all suspicion of causing his death. If the Duke of

Guise were made away with, you will be free of all suspicion concerning him."

The attendant, who had already created the document that King Henry III wanted, handed it to him.

King Henry III said to the Duke of Epernoun, "First let us set our signature and seal to this, and then I'll tell you what I mean to do."

He wrote his signature, sealed the document, and ordered the attendant, "So, convey this to the council immediately."

The attendant exited with the document.

King Henry III of France then said, "And, Epernoun, although I seem mild and calm, think only that I am tragical within — I am willing to act in such a way as to cause death.

"I'll secretly go to the city of Blois on the Loire River, for now that Paris takes the Duke of Guise's part, here is no place for the King of France to stay, unless he intends to be betrayed and die.

"But, as I live, I swear that surely the Duke of Guise shall die."

CHAPTER 21

[SCENE TWENTY-ONE]

With his friend Bartus present, the King of Navarre read a letter.

The King of Navarre said, "My lord, I am informed from France that the Duke of Guise has taken up arms against King Henry III of France and that Paris has revolted against the King."

"Then your grace has a fit and appropriate opportunity to show your love and respect to the King of France," Bartus said. "You can offer him aid against his enemies. This aid cannot but be thankfully received."

"Bartus, it shall be so," the King of Navarre said. "Ride posthaste, then, to France, and there salute his highness King Henry III in our name. Assure him that we will provide all the aid we can against the Guisians and their accomplices. Bartus, leave. Commend me to his grace, and tell him that before long, I'll visit him."

"I will, my lord," Bartus said as he exited.

The King of Navarre called, "Pleshé!"

His friend Pleshé entered the room.

"Pleshé, go muster up our men with speed," the King of Navarre ordered, "and let them march away to France in full force, at full speed, and without delay, for we must aid King Henry III against the Duke of Guise. Leave, I say; it is time that we were there."

"I go, my lord," Pleshé said as he exited.

Alone, the King of Navarre said to himself, "I very much fear that the wicked Duke of Guise will be the ruin of that famous realm of France, for his aspiring, ambitious thoughts aim at the crown and he takes his vantage-ground on religion, to plant the Pope and Popelings — the Pope's followers, especially priests — in the realm, and bind it wholly to the See of Rome.

"But if God will prosper my attempts and send us safely to France, we'll beat the Duke of Guise back, and drive him to his death, that man who basely seeks the ruin of his realm."

CHAPTER 22

King Henry III had been afraid that the Duke of Guise had much support from the King of Spain, but following the decisive defeat of the Spanish Armada by the English navy during the summer of 1588, he feared that support much less.

On 23 December 1588, Cossin, who was the Captain of the Guard, talked with three murderers in the room outside the King's private chamber.

"Come on, sirs," he said, "are you resolutely determined, you who hate the life and honor of the Duke of Guise? Won't you be afraid when you see him come?"

The first murderer replied, "Fear him, you said? Tush, if he were here, we would kill him immediately."

"Oh, I wish that his heart were beating and leaping in my hand!" the second murderer said.

"But when will he come, so that we may murder him?" the third murderer asked.

"Well, then," Cossin said, "I see that you are resolute and will kill him."

"Let us alone," the first murderer said. "Leave it to us. I promise you that you can rely on us."

"Then, sirs, take your standings — your positions — within this chamber for soon the Duke of Guise will come," Cossin said.

The word "standings" brings to mind stands from which hunters shoot game.

"You will give us our money?" the murderers asked.

"Yes, yes, don't be worried about that," Cossin said. "Stand concealed, so, and be resolute."

The three murderers concealed themselves.

Cossin said, "Now falls the star — the Duke of Guise — whose influence governs France, and whose light was deadly to the Protestants. Now must he fall and perish in his height."

King Henry III and the Duke of Epernoun arrived.

King Henry III asked Cossin, "Now, Captain of my Guard, are these murderers ready?"

"They are, my good lord," Cossin replied.

"But are they resolute, and armed to kill, hating the life and honor of the Duke of Guise?" King Henry III asked.

"I promise you that they are, my lord," Cossin replied.

"Then come, proud Duke of Guise, and here empty your breast, which is overburdened with an excess of ambitious thoughts," King Henry III said. "Breathe out that life wherein my death was hidden, and end your endless treasons with your death."

The Duke of Guise knocked at the door leading into this room, and he called, "Holla, page, hey!"

He expected a servant to open the door, which led to a room just outside the King's private chamber, but the Duke of Epernoun opened it.

The Duke of Guise asked, "Epernoun, where is the King?"

"Gone to his royal study," the Duke of Epernoun answered. Actually, the King was still present, but he was on the far side of the room, close to his private chamber.

"Please, tell him that the Duke of Guise is here."

The Duke of Epernoun said to the King, whom he pretended had just entered the room, "If it please your grace, the Duke of Guise asks for access to your highness."

"Let him come in," King Henry III said loudly.

Then he said quietly, "Come, Guise, and see your traitorous guile outmatched. Come, and perish in the pit you made for me."

The Duke of Guise walked over to the King and said, "Good morning to your majesty."

Behind his back, two of the three murderers went into the room that the Duke of Guise had just vacated.

"Good morning to my loving kinsman the Duke of Guise," King Henry III said. "How fares it this morning with your excellence?"

"I heard that your majesty was scarcely pleased that in the court I bore so great a train of attendants," the Duke of Guise replied.

"Those who said I was displeased were to blame; and you, too, good kinsman, are to blame if you imagine that I was displeased," King Henry III said. "It would be distressing if I would doubt my kin, or be suspicious of my dearest friends.

"Kinsman, assure yourself that I am resolute, whatever anyone whispers in my ears, not to suspect disloyalty in you, and so, sweet kinsman, farewell."

King Henry III exited, along with the Duke of Epernoun and Cossin.

The Duke of Guise was still present, as well as one of the three hidden murderers.

"So," the Duke of Guise said, and he paused to think.

Then he said, "Now the King sues for favor to me, the Duke of Guise, and all his minions stoop when I command. Why, this is the result of having an army in the field! Now, by the holy sacrament, I swear that as ancient Romans triumphed over their captive lords, so I will triumph over this wanton, lascivious King Henry III, and he shall follow my proud chariot's wheels."

Victorious ancient Roman generals were given triumphal processions in which they rode in a chariot while their most important prisoners walked, bound and humiliated, behind it.

The Duke of Guise continued:

"Now that I have an army, I begin to look about and see the greatness that is in store for me, and I feel that all my former time was spent in vain because I can now do so much more. Don't break, sword, for in you is the Duke of Guise's hope."

The third murderer revealed himself. He had hidden in a spot close to where the Duke of Guise stood — the two other murderers were in the next room.

The Duke of Guise said, "Villain, why do you look so ghastly? Speak."

The third murderer, who was suffering from an attack of bad conscience, said, "Oh, pardon me, my Lord of Guise!"

"Pardon you?" the Duke of Guise said. "Why, what have you done?"

"Oh, my lord, I am one of them who is set to murder you."

"To murder me, villain?"

"Yes, my lord: the rest have taken their standings in the next room," the third murderer said. "Therefore, my good lord, don't go forth."

"Yet Caesar shall go forth," the Duke of Guise, a very proud man, said. "Let mean imaginations and intellects and baser men fear death! But they are peasants; I am the Duke of Guise, and princes just with their looks engender and produce fear."

The Duke of Guise moved into the next room.

"Stand close," the first murderer said. "The Duke of Guise is coming; I know that it is him by his voice."

The Duke of Guise said about the third murderer's complexion, "As pale as ashes."

Then he said, "So then it is time to look about for danger."

The first and second murderers appeared and said, "Down with him! Down with him!"

The first and second murderers stabbed him.

The third murderer fled or cowered or joined in the murder.

"Oh, I have my death's wound," the Duke of Guise said. "Give me permission to speak."

"Then pray to God, and ask for the forgiveness of the King," the second murderer said.

"Don't bother me," the Duke of Guise said. "I never offended Him, nor will I ask forgiveness of the King. Oh, that I lack the power to save my life, and I lack immortality to be revenged. To die at the hands of peasants, what a grief is this!

"Ah, Pope Sixtus V, be revenged upon King Henry III.

"King Philip II of Spain, I am slain because of working for you and your general, the Duke of Parma.

"Pope Sixtus V, excommunicate the wicked branch of the cursed House of Valois, and King Philip II, depose the wicked branch of the cursed House of Valois!

"*Vive la Messe*! Let the Mass live! May the Huguenots perish!

"Thus Caesar did go forth, and thus he died."

The Duke of Guise died, and Cossin, the Captain of the Guard, entered the room and asked the murderers, "Have you finished? Then stay a while, and I'll go call King Henry III."

King Henry III of France entered the room, and Cossin said, "But look, here he comes."

Accompanying King Henry III were the Duke of Epernoun and some attendants.

Cossin said to the King, "My lord, look, the Duke of Guise has been slain."

King Henry III said, "Ah, this sweet sight is medicine to my soul. Go fetch his son so he can see his father in death."

An attendant exited.

King Henry III continued:

"Overburdened with the guilt of a thousand massacres, Monsieur of Lorraine, sink away to hell!"

By "Monsieur of Lorraine," King Henry III meant the Duke of Guise, who was a member of the House of Lorraine.

King Henry III continued:

"And, in remembrance of those bloody wars, to which you did allure me, while you were alive, and here in presence of you all, I swear, I never was King of France until this hour.

"This is the traitor who has spent my gold in making foreign wars and civil battles.

"Didn't he draw a band of English priests from the seminary at Douai to the seminary at Rheims, in order to hatch forth treason against their natural Queen: Elizabeth of England?

"Didn't he cause the King of Spain's huge fleet — the Armada of 1588 — to threaten England, and to menace me?

"Didn't he injure Monsieur, who is now deceased?"

By "Monsieur," he meant the Duke of Alençon, King Henry III's younger brother. He had been the next in line to the throne of France until he died on 10 June 1584.

King Henry III continued:

"Hasn't he made me — in order to defend the Pope — spend the treasury in civil battles between the King of Navarre and me? That treasury should have been spent to strengthen my land!

"Tush, to be short, the Duke of Guise intended to make me monk, or else to murder me, and so himself become King of France."

By "make me monk," King Henry III meant that the Duke of Guise wanted him to be made poor like a monk who has taken a vow of poverty, or to be sequestered in a monastery almost as if he were a prisoner, or both.

King Henry III continued:

"Let Christian princes, who shall hear of this — all the world shall know that our Duke of Guise is dead — rest satisfied with this, that here I swear that never was there any King of France so yoked — restrained as if I were a beast of burden in a yoke — as I have been."

The Duke of Guise's son entered the room.

The Duke of Epernoun said, "My lord, here is his son."

King Henry III said, "Boy, look where your father lies."

"My father slain! Who has done this deed?"

"Sirrah, it was I who slew him," King Henry III said, "and I will slay you, too, if you prove to be such a traitor as was your father."

The Duke of Guise's son said, "You are the King, and you have done this bloody deed? I'll be revenged."

He started to draw his dagger but was forcibly stopped.

"Away to prison with him!" King Henry III said. "I'll clip his wings before he ever passes out of my hands. Take him away!"

Some guards took the Duke of Guise's son away.

King Henry III continued:

"But what does it matter that this traitor's dead when the Duke of Dumaine, his brother, is alive? And what does it matter that this traitor's dead when the young Cardinal of Lorraine, also his brother, and who has grown so proud, is alive?"

He ordered an attendant, "Go to the Governor of Orleans, and order him, in my name, to kill the Duke of Dumaine."

He then ordered Cossin and the murderers, "Go, now, and strangle the Cardinal of Lorraine."

Cossin and the murderers exited.

King Henry III continued:

"These two — the Duke of Dumaine and the Cardinal of Lorraine — will be as dangerous as one entire Duke of Guise, especially with our old Queen-Mother's help."

Catherine the Queen-Mother entered the room.

"My lord," the Duke of Epernoun said. "Look! See, she is coming, as if she drooped to hear this news."

"So let her droop," King Henry III said. "My heart is light enough."

He then said to her, "Mother, how do you like this plot of mine? I slew the Duke of Guise because I would be King."

"King, why, so you were before," Catherine the Queen-Mother said. "Pray to God that you continue to be a King now this is done!"

"No, the Duke of Guise was King of France," Henry III said, "and he countermanded me and opposed my orders, but now I will be King, and rule myself, and I will make the Guisians who are alive stoop."

"I cannot speak for grief," Catherine the Queen-Mother said. "I wish that I had murdered you when you were born, my son! My son? You are a changeling, and not my son. I curse you, and I proclaim loudly that you are a miscreant, a traitor to God and to the realm of France!"

A changeling is an inferior fairy baby that fairies leave in exchange for a promising human baby.

"Cry out, exclaim, howl until your throat is hoarse," King Henry III said. "The Duke of Guise has been slain, and I rejoice because of it. And now I will go to arms against the Catholic League, which supported the Duke of Guise.

"Come, Epernoun, and let her grieve her heart out, if she will."

King Henry III and the Duke of Epernoun exited.

"Go away, leave me alone to meditate," Catherine the Queen-Mother ordered the attendants, who exited.

Alone, Catherine the Queen-Mother said this:

"Sweet Guise, I wish that my son the King would have died as long as you were here and still alive. To whom shall I reveal my secrets now, and who will help to build religion?

"The Protestants will glory and insultingly exult in their victory. The wicked King of Navarre will get the crown of France. The Popedom cannot last; all goes to ruin.

"And all because of your death, my Guise! What may I do?

"But sorrow seizes upon my toiling soul, for since the Duke of Guise is dead, I will not live."

She died not long after, on 5 January 1589.

CHAPTER 23

[SCENE TWENTY-THREE]

On 24 December 1588, two murderers — the third murderer was not present — seized the Cardinal of Lorraine, one of the Duke of Guise's brothers.

"Don't murder me," he said. "I am a Cardinal."

"Even if you were the Pope," the first murderer said, "you would not escape from us."

"Will you defile your hands with churchmen's blood?" the Cardinal of Lorraine asked.

"Shed your blood?" the second murderer said. "Oh, lord, no, for we intend to strangle you."

"Then there is no remedy, and I must die," the Cardinal of Lorraine said.

"No remedy," the first murderer agreed, "and therefore prepare yourself."

"My brother the Duke of Dumaine still lives, and many others do, who will avenge our deaths — mine and my brother's — upon that cursed King Henry III, upon whose heart may all the Furies seize and with their paws submerge, drench, and drown his black soul in hell!"

"Your black soul, my Lord Cardinal, you should have said," the first murderer said.

The two murderers strangled him.

"So, pull on the cord with full force," the first murderer said. "He is hardhearted; therefore, pull with violence."

The Cardinal of Lorraine died, and the first murderer said, "Come, take him away."

CHAPTER 24

[SCENE TWENTY-FOUR]

The Duke of Dumaine was reading a letter. Some attendants were present.

He said, "My noble brother the Duke of Guise murdered by King Henry III! Oh, what may I do to revenge your death? The King's death by itself cannot provide satisfaction.

"Sweet Duke of Guise, our prop to lean upon, now that you are dead, here there is no support for us.

"I am your brother, and I'll revenge your death, and root the House of Valois out of France; and beat that proud member of the House of Bourbon — the King of Navarre — back to his native home. The King of Navarre basely seeks to join with such a King — Henry III — whose murderous thoughts will be the King of Navarre's overthrow.

"King Henry III ordered the Governor of Orleans, in his name, to make sure that I speedily should have been put to death. But that's been prevented by precautionary measures, leaving me free to end the life of King Henry III and the lives of all those traitors to the Church of Rome who dared to attempt to murder noble Guise."

A Friar entered and said, "My lord, I come to bring you news that your brother the Cardinal of Lorraine, by King Henry III's consent, was recently strangled to death."

"My brother the Cardinal is slain, and I am still alive?" the Duke of Dumaine said. "Oh, words of power that could kill a thousand men!"

He said to his attendants, "Come, let us go and levy men. It is war that must allay this tyrant's pride."

The Friar said, "My lord, hear me speak. I am a Friar of the order of the Jacobins."

He was a French member of the Dominican order. They were called Jacobins because the Church of St. Jacques (aka Saint Jacobus, aka Saint

James) in Paris had been given to them. Near this church, they built their first monastery.

The Friar continued, "I for my conscience's sake will kill the King."

"But what moves you, more than what you have said, to do the deed?" the Duke of Dumaine asked.

"Oh, my lord," the Friar said, "I have been a great sinner in my days, and the deed is meritorious."

"But how will you get the opportunity to kill King Henry III?"

"Tush, my lord, let me alone for that," the Friar said. "Leave that to me."

"Friar, come with me," the Duke of Dumaine said. "We will go talk more about this in a more private place."

CHAPTER 25

King Henry III of France, the King of Navarre, the Duke of Epernoun, Bartus, and Pleshé stood together. Some soldiers and attendants were also present.

In 1589, King Henry III of France and the King of Navarre were fighting on the same side. After the murder of the Duke of Guise, the Pope and the Sorbonne no longer recognized Henry III as the rightful King of France. Right now, King Henry III and the King of Navarre were besieging Paris.

King Henry III said, "Brother of Navarre, I sorrow much that I ever proved to be your enemy."

Kings often called each other "brother" despite not being biologically related. Kings also called Queens "sister."

He continued, "And I sorrow much that the sweet and princely mind you bear was ever troubled with injurious wars. I vow, as I am lawful King of France, to recompense your reconciled love with all the honors and affections that I have always bestowed upon my dearest friends."

"It is enough if I, the King of Navarre, may be esteemed faithful to the King of France, who may always command my service until death."

"I give thanks to my kingly brother of Navarre," King Henry III said. "Here then we'll camp before the walls of Lutetia."

Lutetia Parisiorum is the old Latin name of Paris.

He continued, "We will encircle this strumpet — unfaithful to her rightful King — city with our siege, until, surfeiting with our afflicting arms, she casts her hateful and hate-full stomach to the earth."

The image was of Paris vomiting out hate after getting more than her fill of warfare.

A messenger arrived and said to King Henry III, "If it pleases your majesty, here is a friar of the order of the Jacobins, sent from the President of Paris, who craves access to your grace."

The President of Paris is the head of the Parlement or local assembly. He is the appointed Governor of Paris.

"Let him come in," King Henry III ordered.

The friar, carrying a letter, arrived.

"I don't like this friar's look," the Duke of Epernoun said. "It would not be amiss, my lord, if he were searched."

"Sweet Epernoun, our friars are holy men, and will not offer violence to their King, for all the wealth and treasure of the world," King Henry III replied.

He then asked, "Friar, do you acknowledge me as your rightful King?"

He asked that because so many people in Paris were now not regarding him as their rightful King.

"Yes, my good lord, and I will die therein," the friar replied.

The words "will die therein" were equivocal and could mean either die for the King or die opposing the King. The word "yes' was equivocal in the sense of either he was telling the truth or he was lying when he acknowledged Henry III to be his rightful King.

"Then come near, and tell me what news you bring," King Henry III said.

The friar came near and said, "My lord, the appointed Governor of Paris greets your grace and sends his duty by these hastily written lines, humbly craving your gracious reply."

He gave the King of France the note.

"I'll read the lines of writing, friar, and then I'll answer you," King Henry III said.

"*Sancte Jacobus*, now have mercy upon me!" the friar prayed.

He stabbed King Henry III with a knife as the King was reading the letter. King Henry III fought back, got possession of the knife, and stabbed the friar.

"Oh, my lord, let him live a while!" the Duke of Epernoun said.

He wanted the friar to be tortured.

King Henry III stabbed the friar again and said, "No, let the villain die, and feel in hell just torments for his treachery."

The friar died.

"What!" the King of Navarre said, seeing blood on King Henry III. "Is your highness hurt?"

"Yes, I am, Navarre, but not to death, I hope," King Henry III said.

"May God shield your grace from such a sudden death!" the King of Navarre said.

He ordered an attendant, "Go call a surgeon hither straightaway."

"What irreligious pagans' acts be these, by such men who believe themselves to be members of the holy church?" King Henry III said. "Take away that damned villain from my sight!"

Attendants carried out the friar's body.

"Ah, if your highness had let him live," the Duke of Epernoun said, "we might have punished him to the full extent of his deserts."

"Sweet Epernoun, all rebels under heaven shall learn from the example of his punishment how they should think about bearing arms against their sovereign," King Henry III replied.

He then ordered, "Go call the English ambassador to France to come here immediately."

An attendant exited.

King Henry III then said, "I'll send my sister Elizabeth the Queen of England news of this, and give her warning about her treacherous foes."

A surgeon arrived.

"Does it please your grace to let the surgeon examine your wound?" the King of Navarre asked.

Part of the examination was probing the wound to see how deep and serious it is.

"The wound, I promise you, is deep, my lord," King Henry III said.

He added, "Probe and examine it, surgeon, and tell me what you see."

As the surgeon probed the wound, the English ambassador arrived.

King Henry III said, "English ambassador, send your Queen word of what this detested Jacobin has done. Tell her, for all this, that I hope to live. If I do live, the papal monarch will go to wrack and ruin, and the anti-Christian kingdom will fall. These bloody hands shall tear the Pope's triple crown, and set on fire accursed Rome about his ears. I'll set on fire his crazed, shaky, unsound buildings, and incense — consume with fire — the papal towers until they kiss the lowly earth."

He then said, "Navarre, give me your hand. I here do swear to ruinate that wicked church of Rome, which hatches such bloody plots and conspiracies. And here I profess eternal love to you, and to the Queen of England specially, whom God has blessed for hating papistry."

"These words revive my thoughts, and comfort me," the King of Navarre said. "It is comforting to see your highness in this virtuous mind."

"Tell me, surgeon, shall I live?" King Henry III asked.

"Unfortunately, my lord, the wound is dangerous," the surgeon replied, "for you have been stricken with a poisoned knife."

"A poisoned knife!" Henry III said. "Shall I, the French King, die, both wounded and poisoned at the same time?"

"Oh, I wish that that damned villain were alive again, so that we might torture him with some newly invented way of causing death," the Duke of Epernoun said.

"He died a death too good," Bartus said. "May the devil of hell torture his wicked soul!"

"Ah, don't curse him, since he is dead," King Henry III said. "Oh, the fatal poison works within my breast. Tell me, surgeon, and don't lie to me — may I live?"

"I am sorry to say, my lord," the surgeon said, "that your highness cannot live."

"Surgeon, why do you say that?" the King of Navarre said. "The King may live."

"Oh, no, Navarre," King Henry III said. "I must die, and you must be King of France!"

"Long may you live, and still be King of France," the King of Navarre said.

The Duke of Epernoun said, "If you don't live, I pray that I, Epernoun, may die!"

"Sweet Epernoun, your King must die," Henry III said. "My lords, fight on the side of this valiant prince, Navarre, for he is your lawful King, and my next heir.

"Valois' line ends in my tragedy. Now let the House of Bourbon wear the crown, and may it never end in blood, as mine has done."

King Henry III was the last Valois King of France. Navarre, who would be crowned Henry IV, would be the first Bourbon King of France.

King Henry III continued:

"Weep not, sweet Navarre, but revenge my death.

"Ah, Epernoun, is this your love to me? Henry, your King, wipes off these childish tears, and bids you to whet your sword on Pope Sixtus V's bones, so that it may keenly slice the Catholics."

To sharpen his sword on Pope Sixtus V's bones, Epernoun would have to kill him first.

Henry V continued:

"He does not love me the most who sheds the most tears; he loves me the most who makes the most lavish outpouring of his blood in the fight against the Catholics.

"Set on fire Paris, where these treacherous rebels lurk.

"I die, Navarre; come carry me to my sepulcher. Salute the Queen of England in my name, and tell her that Henry III dies her faithful friend."

King Henry III died.

The King of Navarre, soon to be crowned King Henry IV of France, said, "Come, lords, take up the body of the King, so that we may see it honorably interred. And then I vow to so revenge his death that Rome, and all those popish prelates there, shall curse the time that ever Navarre was King of France and ruled there because of King Henry III's fateful death."

They marched out. The body of King Henry III lay on four men's shoulders. A solemn march played, and as they marched out, the attendants held their pikes near the spearhead and let the shafts drag on the ground.

APPENDIX A: ABOUT THE AUTHOR

It was a dark and stormy night. Suddenly a cry rang out, and on a hot summer night in 1954, Josephine, wife of Carl Bruce, gave birth to a boy — me. Unfortunately, this young married couple allowed Reuben Saturday, Josephine's brother, to name their first-born. Reuben, aka "The Joker," decided that Bruce was a nice name, so he decided to name me Bruce Bruce. I have gone by my middle name — David — ever since.

Being named Bruce David Bruce hasn't been all bad. Bank tellers remember me very quickly, so I don't often have to show an ID. It can be fun in charades, also. When I was a counselor as a teenager at Camp Echoing Hills in Warsaw, Ohio, a fellow counselor gave the signs for "sounds like" and "two words," then she pointed to a bruise on her leg twice. Bruise Bruise? Oh yeah, Bruce Bruce is the answer!

Uncle Reuben, by the way, gave me a haircut when I was in kindergarten. He cut my hair short and shaved a small bald spot on the back of my head. My mother wouldn't let me go to school until the bald spot grew out again.

Of all my brothers and sisters (six in all), I am the only transplant to Athens, Ohio. I was born in Newark, Ohio, and have lived all around Southeastern Ohio. However, I moved to Athens to go to Ohio University and have never left.

At Ohio U, I never could make up my mind whether to major in English or Philosophy, so I got a bachelor's degree with a double major in both areas, then I added a Master of Arts degree in English and a Master of Arts degree in Philosophy. Yes, I have my MAMA degree.

Currently, and for a long time to come (I eat fruits and veggies), I am spending my retirement writing books such as *Nadia Comaneci: Perfect 10*, *The Funniest People in Dance*, *Homer's* Iliad: *A Retelling in Prose*, and *William Shakespeare's* Othello: *A Retelling in Prose*.

By the way, my sister Brenda Kennedy writes romances such as *A New Beginning* and *Shattered Dreams*.

APPENDIX B: SOME BOOKS BY DAVID BRUCE

Retellings of a Classic Work of Literature

Arden of Faversham*: A Retelling*

Ben Jonson's The Alchemist: *A Retelling*

Ben Jonson's The Arraignment, or Poetaster: *A Retelling*

Ben Jonson's Bartholomew Fair: *A Retelling*

Ben Jonson's The Case is Altered: *A Retelling*

Ben Jonson's Catiline's Conspiracy: *A Retelling*

Ben Jonson's The Devil is an Ass: *A Retelling*

Ben Jonson's Epicene: *A Retelling*

Ben Jonson's Every Man in His Humor: *A Retelling*

Ben Jonson's Every Man Out of His Humor: *A Retelling*

Ben Jonson's The Fountain of Self-Love, or Cynthia's Revels: *A Retelling*

Ben Jonson's The Magnetic Lady, or Humors Reconciled: *A Retelling*

Ben Jonson's The New Inn, or The Light Heart: *A Retelling*

Ben Jonson's Sejanus' Fall: *A Retelling*

Ben Jonson's The Staple of News: *A Retelling*

Ben Jonson's A Tale of a Tub: *A Retelling*

Ben Jonson's Volpone, or the Fox: *A Retelling*

Christopher Marlowe's Complete Plays: Retellings

Christopher Marlowe's Dido, Queen of Carthage: *A Retelling*

Christopher Marlowe's Doctor Faustus: *Retellings of the 1604 A-Text and of the 1616 B-Text*

Christopher Marlowe's Edward II: *A Retelling*

Christopher Marlowe's The Massacre at Paris: *A Retelling*

Christopher Marlowe's The Rich Jew of Malta: *A Retelling*

Christopher Marlowe's Tamburlaine, Parts 1 and 2: *Retellings*

Dante's Divine Comedy: *A Retelling in Prose*

Dante's Inferno: *A Retelling in Prose*

Dante's Purgatory: *A Retelling in Prose*

Dante's Paradise: *A Retelling in Prose*

The Famous Victories of Henry V: *A Retelling*

From the Iliad *to the* Odyssey: *A Retelling in Prose of Quintus of Smyrna's* Posthomerica

George Chapman, Ben Jonson, and John Marston's Eastward Ho! *A Retelling*

George Peele's The Arraignment of Paris: *A Retelling*

George Peele's The Battle of Alcazar: *A Retelling*

George Peele's David and Bathsheba, and the Tragedy of Absalom: *A Retelling*

George Peele's Edward I: *A Retelling*

George Peele's The Old Wives' Tale: *A Retelling*

George-a-Greene: *A Retelling*

The History of King Leir: *A Retelling*

Homer's Iliad: *A Retelling in Prose*

Homer's Odyssey: *A Retelling in Prose*

J.W. Gent.'s The Valiant Scot: *A Retelling*

Jason and the Argonauts: A Retelling in Prose of Apollonius of Rhodes' Argonautica

John Ford: Eight Plays Translated into Modern English

John Ford's The Broken Heart: *A Retelling*

John Ford's The Fancies, Chaste and Noble: *A Retelling*

John Ford's The Lady's Trial: *A Retelling*

John Ford's The Lover's Melancholy: *A Retelling*

John Ford's Love's Sacrifice: *A Retelling*

John Ford's Perkin Warbeck: *A Retelling*

John Ford's The Queen: *A Retelling*

John Ford's 'Tis Pity She's a Whore: *A Retelling*

John Lyly's Campaspe: *A Retelling*

John Lyly's Endymion, The Man in the Moon: *A Retelling*

John Lyly's Galatea: *A Retelling*

John Lyly's Love's Metamorphosis: *A Retelling*

John Lyly's Midas: *A Retelling*

John Lyly's Mother Bombie: *A Retelling*

John Lyly's Sappho and Phao: *A Retelling*

John Lyly's The Woman in the Moon: *A Retelling*

John Webster's The White Devil: *A Retelling*

King Edward III: *A Retelling*

Mankind: *A Medieval Morality Play* (A Retelling)

Margaret Cavendish's The Unnatural Tragedy: *A Retelling*

The Merry Devil of Edmonton: *A Retelling*

The Summoning of Everyman: *A Medieval Morality Play* (A Retelling)

Robert Greene's Friar Bacon and Friar Bungay: *A Retelling*

The Taming of a Shrew: *A Retelling*

Tarlton's Jests: A Retelling

Thomas Middleton's A Chaste Maid in Cheapside: *A Retelling*

Thomas Middleton's Women Beware Women: *A Retelling*

Thomas Middleton and Thomas Dekker's The Roaring Girl: *A Retelling*
Thomas Middleton and William Rowley's The Changeling: *A Retelling*
The Trojan War and Its Aftermath: Four Ancient Epic Poems
Virgil's Aeneid: *A Retelling in Prose*
William Shakespeare's 5 Late Romances: Retellings in Prose
William Shakespeare's 10 Histories: Retellings in Prose
William Shakespeare's 11 Tragedies: Retellings in Prose
William Shakespeare's 12 Comedies: Retellings in Prose
William Shakespeare's 38 Plays: Retellings in Prose
William Shakespeare's 1 Henry IV, aka Henry IV, Part 1: *A Retelling in Prose*
William Shakespeare's 2 Henry IV, aka Henry IV, Part 2: *A Retelling in Prose*
William Shakespeare's 1 Henry VI, aka Henry VI, Part 1: *A Retelling in Prose*
William Shakespeare's 2 Henry VI, aka Henry VI, Part 2: *A Retelling in Prose*
William Shakespeare's 3 Henry VI, aka Henry VI, Part 3: *A Retelling in Prose*
William Shakespeare's All's Well that Ends Well: *A Retelling in Prose*
William Shakespeare's Antony and Cleopatra: *A Retelling in Prose*
William Shakespeare's As You Like It: *A Retelling in Prose*
William Shakespeare's The Comedy of Errors: *A Retelling in Prose*
William Shakespeare's Coriolanus: *A Retelling in Prose*
William Shakespeare's Cymbeline: *A Retelling in Prose*
William Shakespeare's Hamlet: *A Retelling in Prose*
William Shakespeare's Henry V: *A Retelling in Prose*
William Shakespeare's Henry VIII: *A Retelling in Prose*
William Shakespeare's Julius Caesar: *A Retelling in Prose*
William Shakespeare's King John: *A Retelling in Prose*
William Shakespeare's King Lear: *A Retelling in Prose*
William Shakespeare's Love's Labor's Lost: *A Retelling in Prose*
William Shakespeare's Macbeth: *A Retelling in Prose*
William Shakespeare's Measure for Measure: *A Retelling in Prose*
William Shakespeare's The Merchant of Venice: *A Retelling in Prose*
William Shakespeare's The Merry Wives of Windsor: *A Retelling in Prose*
William Shakespeare's A Midsummer Night's Dream: *A Retelling in Prose*
William Shakespeare's Much Ado About Nothing: *A Retelling in Prose*
William Shakespeare's Othello: *A Retelling in Prose*
William Shakespeare's Pericles, Prince of Tyre: *A Retelling in Prose*
William Shakespeare's Richard II: *A Retelling in Prose*
William Shakespeare's Richard III: *A Retelling in Prose*
William Shakespeare's Romeo and Juliet: *A Retelling in Prose*
William Shakespeare's The Taming of the Shrew: *A Retelling in Prose*

William Shakespeare's The Tempest: *A Retelling in Prose*
William Shakespeare's Timon of Athens: *A Retelling in Prose*
William Shakespeare's Titus Andronicus: *A Retelling in Prose*
William Shakespeare's Troilus and Cressida: *A Retelling in Prose*
William Shakespeare's Twelfth Night: *A Retelling in Prose*
William Shakespeare's The Two Gentlemen of Verona: *A Retelling in Prose*
William Shakespeare's The Two Noble Kinsmen: *A Retelling in Prose*
William Shakespeare's The Winter's Tale: *A Retelling in Prose*

9 7 9 8 2 0 1 1 3 2 7 0 5